The Cocoa Dancer
and Other Stories

Alwin Bully

D0925178

PAPILLOTE PRESS
London and Trafalgar, Dominica

First published Great Britain in 2021

© Alwin Bully 2021

A CIP catalogue reference for this book is available from the British Library

Cover art Alwin Bully
Book design by Andy Dark
Printed and bound by Imprint Digital, Exeter, UK

ISBN: 978 1 8380415 6 4

Papillote Press
23 Rozel Road,
London SW4 0EY,
United Kingdom
And Trafalgar, Dominica
www.papillotepress.co.uk

The Cocoa Dancer and Other Stories has been produced by the Papillote People's Press, a book production company under the Papillote Press imprint.

For my parents, my father Charles Emmanuel Bully,
who knew and loved our Dominican stories and
legends; and my mother Ena Louise Potter Bully,
who knew how to tell them.

Other works by the same author

SOME STORIES FROM THIS BOOK FIRST APPEARED IN THE FOLLOWING
PUBLICATIONS:

'Jonkunnu Story' (*The Caribbean Writer: The Literary Gem of the Caribbean*,
volume 25, 2011)

'Parting' (*Iron Balloons: Hit Fiction from Jamaica's Calabash Writers Workshop*, edited
by Colin Channer, 2006, Colin Channer/Calabash International Literary Festival)

'The Cocoa Dancer' (*BIM: Arts for the 21st Century*, volume 3, No.1,
Errol Barrow Center for the Creative Imagination, UWI Cave Hill & Government
of Barbados, 2009)

'The Man Who Loved Clocks' (*BIM: Arts for the 21st Century*, volume 5, No.2,
Errol Barrow Center for the Creative Imagination, UWI Cave Hill & Government
of Barbados, 2012)

'A Toothbrush for Christmas' (Waitukubuli Writers: *Montage Domnik*, River Ridge
Press, Dominica, 2021)

Praise for Alwin Bully

Alwin Bully has been a luminary of world literature for decades. With this collection, he is allowing us into the attic and cellar of his imagination, where he has stored astonishing histories and legacies. We are all the richer for his generosity, grace, and for the artistic impulse beating at these stories' heart. COLIN CHANNER

Spanning some five decades, the ten stories can make us laugh at the characters or in recognition of our own selves. They can move us and surprise us in their dramatic unravelling. Bully's remarkable ear allows him to render the vernaculars of Caribbean speech, wherever these stories happen — Jamaica, Barbados, Trinidad, St Lucia and his own Dominica. What remains constant, however, is the historical consciousness of the Caribbean that drives an ultimate optimism. This collection is one of victory over historical suffering, political apocalypse and personal tragedy. There can be no more urgent time for this message than now. RAWLE GIBBONS

The Cocoa Dancer and Other Stories comes from the imagination and creativity of the foremost Caribbean artiste of his generation. It is a product of the same story-telling brilliance that has crafted numerous plays and films for our education and entertainment. The stories bear the same sense of appreciation and love for our social and physical environment evident in all his art. Excellent! DORBRENE E O'MARRE

These stories speak eloquently of a rich Caribbean cultural milieu of myth, superstition, racial prejudice, cultural recuperation, embodied resistance, familial loss, and existential transcendence against the pervasive machinery of time. Bully's narrative weave is animated with delectable prose, vivid poetic imagery and spare seasoning of vernacular language that shape dramatic event, situation and character with compelling immediacy and a warm universal humanity. EUGENE F WILLIAMS

CONTENTS

INTRODUCTION

Alwin Bully's curriculum vitae is an impressive record of a life dedicated to the arts, cultural administration and education. An inspiration to several generations of Caribbean theatre persons, he has been playwright (with at least 16 plays to his credit), actor, director (both theatre and film), costume designer (with awards from carnival organisers), stage and lighting designer, graphic artist, painter, sculptor, illustrator, composer, art teacher, and film maker.

With his early education in Dominica, at the Dominica Grammar School and St Mary's Academy, he graduated from the Cave Hill campus of the University of the West Indies with a BA, General Honours. In 2011, UWI awarded him an honorary Doctorate of Letters.

He was a founding member of several Dominican arts and cultural organisations as well as the Barbados National Theatre Workshop. He distinguished himself during his undergraduate years in Barbados as President of the Guild of Undergraduates and as a regional artist making a substantial contribution to theatre development. He directed and acted in theatre there, taught workshops and was one of the most influential Caribbean theatre people in Barbados during that time. Under the leadership of doyenne Daphne Joseph-Hackett, he travelled as actor with the Barbados Theatre Workshop to several islands.

Back home after studies, he founded the influential People's Action Theatre and was its Artistic Director from 1972-1987. The group's work marked some of the most productive years in Dominican theatre. They travelled to several islands with plays written by Alwin. Among his now classic Dominican plays are *Good Morning Miss Millie* (1968), *Streak* (1977), *The Ruler* (1976), *The Nite Box* (1977), *Pio-Pio* (1978). Many of the plays have been published in anthologies and performed widely.

Alongside his involvement in the arts, he rose in the education system to become acting Principal of the Dominican Grammar School. He later moved on to establish the Department of Culture and became its first Director. At independence, in 1978, he designed the distinctive Dominica National Flag.

His contribution to Caribbean theatre and cultural development is highly respected. He was President of the Caribbean Theatre Information Exchange. Professionally, in 1987, he moved to Jamaica to work at UNESCO as Senior Programme Specialist and later the Caribbean Culture Advisor. There he managed the production of the substantial and ground-breaking six-volume History of the Caribbean. He became deeply involved with theatre in Jamaica and directed several successful award-winning theatre productions, including many of Fr. Richard Ho Lung's popular annual musical dramas.

In 2008 he returned to Dominica as Cultural Advisor to the Minister of Culture and continued his work in theatre and cultural administration. He was the founder and director of the Nature Island Literary Festival. He wrote and directed films, including his *Oseyi and the Masqueraders* in 2017. He has received the National Sisserou Award from the Government of Dominica.

THE STORIES
While Alwin Bully is well known throughout the Caribbean arts and culture world he may not be as well-known as a short-story writer. This collection published by Papillote Press will bring welcome attention to this area of his work.

The Cocoa Dancer and Other Stories gathers ten stories, written between 1968 and 2020. A number have appeared in literary journals like BIM and The Caribbean Writer. Understandably, given the range of years, some stories are more accomplished than others. Set in various Caribbean spaces, touching on various themes — last days of colonialism, masquerade culture, city life, island ethnic tensions, among others — Bully provides a valuable tapestry that records in its weavings, closely observed island cultures and the lives that inhabit these. Except very indirectly, the larger outside world does not intrude.

As with every anthology, we will have favourites, fiction that holds attention through the conflicts, characterisations, capture of cultural-historical moments, within the shaping and framework of story.

The title story is set at the ending of the colonial era, with its plantation capitalism and total authoritarianism of land owners. But the cocoa dancer relates how he set up resistance to the cruelty of the owner of the cocoa field. The estate eventually collapses, the master dies and with the arrival of a relative from England, the dancer eventually inherits the land. In a cyclical turn of events, the narrator turns out to be a descendant of the former owner.

Jonkunnu Story (2011) is a fabulist/marvellous realism type of narrative that utilises the masquerade figures of the Bahamas to place contemporary ecological concerns of the Caribbean in the frame. In making tensions between the folk story characters responsible for the disastrous situation, Bully points to human failure for the environmental degradations we now face.

The River Flows On (1968) reminds us of the divisions that once existed between indigenous and African peoples of Dominica. As they did, and perhaps still do between descendants of African, East Indian and European Caribbean citizens. It is a love story that is frustrated and ended by implacable prejudices of tribe leaders.

The accomplished dramatist and playwright that Bully is turns up in a well-woven crime thriller titled *Lizards Don't Lie* (2006). It uses the modern setting of Jamaican Rastas, middle-class persons, jealousy and the indefinable folk beliefs of the interpenetration of the lives of human and other fauna, like lizards. Read closely and you see how he has blocked and set up the final denouement with the eye of an experienced director.

The Man Who Loved Clocks has a touch of the marvellous about it as with Latin American stories. Other stories explore men-women relationships in different social environments, from academic and commercial (*Showdown in Bridgetown*, 2020) to ghetto (*Woman, Woman*, 1968). He tries his hand at farce in *Cochie's Pwi-Pwi* (1969).

There are some pieces that seem rooted in personal experience, like *A Toothbrush for Christma*s (2020). A similar story, perhaps one of the best in this collection, is *Parting* (2006). At the centre is the lingering anguish of a father who has lost a son and religious faith, and is met by someone who seems to channel the reassurances of the dead son in the midst of a social gathering.

It is good to have this collection of stories from Alwin Bully. Papillote Press is commended as they continue to publish the writers of Dominica (past and present) and other islands of the Caribbean.

JOHN ROBERT LEE

The Cocoa Dancer

I met him on my second visit to St Lucia in the summer of '82. He lived in a small coastal village by the name of Brydens, a few miles outside the capital, and I was told that he was the oldest man on the island — over a hundred and ten years old. His eyesight was failing and he moved slowly but apart from that he had all his wits about him. He spoke loudly and clearly, as if he had an important message to deliver and was anxious to do so before it was too late. So he delivered it to all who would listen, striving to make himself perfectly understood, in the hope that some day somebody would grasp the significance of what he was saying.

I first saw him one Sunday afternoon when I was driving round the island looking for a beach that everyone said was the finest on the island but was still "undiscovered". I knew that story well; I had heard it several times in many places so I wasn't too interested in doing "the tourist thing" of hunting down the island's "best kept secret". No one bothered me too much either as I easily passed for a local — once I kept my mouth shut. So instead of a beach, my drive that afternoon resulted more in a discovery of several fascinating, fragile villages and hamlets along the twisting road, some perched on cliffs overhanging the sea, others at the foot of wide slopes on cream-sanded beaches with the water lapping at their toes.

It was journey of rediscovery of self too, as the landscape triggered memories of family stories on estates in the islands, colonial times and the "bad ole days". The real discovery of the day, however, was the old man of this village who everyone called…the Cocoa Dancer.

He was sitting out front with his feet resting on a little stool in front of him, in the cool afternoon shade of his house, as if on display — like some fragile and important exhibit but one which the village knew so well that no one really took any notice. Yet, there was something about him — the way he stared fixedly at one spot for long periods of time before shifting his gaze. What thoughts were behind those eyes? What treasure-trove of memories was stored within that gray head? I was intrigued.

I drove to the village on three consecutive afternoons to observe him. Each day he was there — sitting in the shadow of his house staring at the ghosts of his past. On the fourth afternoon, I asked a man across the street who he was.

"Who? The Cocoa Dancer? Why you don't ask him yourself?" the man asked with a smirk. "Come mek me mek you meet him."

The first thing you noticed about the Cocoa Dancer was his feet. They were big and soft and covered with the smoothest and most velvety black skin I had ever seen. Each toe was perfectly shaped and capped with a well-cropped pink toenail that gently took the rounded shape of the front of the toe. The arch was rather low for a dancer and the foot bottom was flatter than one would have expected but it, too, was soft and spongy and shrimp-coloured in the purest shades of light oranges mixed with touches of pink, soft reds and a creamish yellow that my mother used to call rose-petal. The heel was large and formed a perfect orb at the back of his foot — like a new cricket ball. His ankles were wide and strong but the bones were covered with such thick layers of muscle that they merged with the general shape of the foot and were hardly visible at the sides. The skin had hardly a wrinkle. They were the most perfect pair of feet I had ever seen. They deserved to be resting on that stool. I soon realised that, in fact, it was they, not the man himself, which were on display. And here is the reason why:

"I used to dance the cocoa," he declared suddenly before I could properly introduce myself. "I started when I was eight years old. Dey would put me to stan' up bare foot in the big iron *tache*, you know the ones they used to boil the molasses in? You can still see dem round de old estates — people paying plenty money for dem now I hear. Well, after the cocoa beans would dry out for three weeks dey used to put me to stan' up in dis big *tache* and pour the cocoa beans in with me, reaching almost to me knees. Then the drummer would start to play and I would dance the cocoa. I had to hold on to the side of the *tache* to support my weight and dance on the cocoa, moving my feet round and round, up and down, as fast as I could to make the cocoa beans turn in the *tache*. Dat way they would get polish — lose all de dry skin dat was on dem and start to turn brown and shiny. Dat is how you get the cocoa ready to use. I had to dance each batch of beans for three hours. Wasn't easy! De drum would give me de riddim and the dancing would help mek time pass quicker but it was hard work still and I hated it.

People used to stop to watch me dance, bright grins on dem face and nodding their heads in time with the drum. Sometimes dey couldn't resist the riddim and would pick up the dance too, trying to follow my movement and commenting on how wonderful me could dance. But I just used to put me face vex-vex and glare back at dem, especially when me friend dem woulda come, and worse when Busha Bryden would come and sit down on him long veranda and watch me, watch me.

One day my mother go up to Busha and say, "Busha, why is Alpheus one you choose to dance de cocoa? Is hard on him and he not getting to go to school. Why you cannot use some of de other boys on de estate?"

Busha stan-up an' give her one box cross she face. She fall down and blood come out de side of she mouth. "Don't try an' tell me how to run my business," Busha say. "You dyam rude an outa order. Get back in the cocoa field and don't come back in me house again unless I send for you."

When my mother tell me what happen I decide that I not dancing de cocoa again. The next morning instead of going to the cocoa shed I stay and sit down in front our shack with my two long foot stretch out on a box just like how I sit now. When de overseer come an' look for me, me say, "Busha beat my mother so me nah work."

"Busha have de right to beat who him want," de overseer say.

"An' me have de right to work when me want," I say. "Busha don't pay me."

"He pay you mother. Dat mean he pay you. He own dis house ounoo living in."

"Dat don't mean him can beat me mudda. Me nah work!"

Two hours later Busha self come down. When me mudda hear him come she step outa de shack and stan up by de door. Busha say, "I hear you refusing to work today, Alpheus. What's the problem?"

"You beat me mudda, so me nah work," I say.

"Alpheus," he say. "You don't work. You dance. It is a privilege. You are the only boy on the estate who wears shoes."

"Me nah want no shoe. De other boy dem laugh after me and say me foot soft an me cyan play ball or run like dem because me have to wear shoe all de time."

"It's because of your work," Busha say.

"Me did tink you say me nah work," I tell Busha. He smile an' pause a while, watching me up and down. Den he say, "You're very rude for a twelve year old."

"A rudeness mek me," me say.

Busha laugh, "Cyah, cyah, cyah." Den him get serious. "Very well," he say, "You nah work. Your mother neither. An' since ounoo is no longer workers on dis estate, you can no longer live here. I want ounoo out of here by tonight. Rupert," he say to de overseer, "See to it. And get one of the other boys to dance de cocoa from today." Den he turn him back an' strut outa we yard. I watch me mudda. She watch me. Den she turn an' go back in de house. When I follow her inside I meet her sitting down on de bed crying. She look on my foot an' say, "Put you shoe on you foot."

"Me don't have to keep me foot clean again," me say. "Me done dance de cocoa."

"Dis man own everyting round here," Mama say. "If we leave we will have nothing."

"Me cyan go back," me say. "Me hate dis man. Me hate how he treat you. Me hate de way he does sit on his veranda and watch me dance the cocoa every day."

"Dere is a reason for dat," she say. I watch her. "He is your father. I is one of his woman dem. If I leave he will destroy me. He tell me so already."

"But he just…"

"Doh mind dat. If I leave he will do it. He do it already. To Liza, me sister. An' to Hotense, who used to dry de cocoa. You wouldn't remember dem. You was still small. Go back an' dance de cocoa, boy. Is your fate, is what God put you here to do. An' believe me, it have much harder jobs dan dat on dis estate."

Was hard but me go back. For me mudda sake. For six more long years me dance de cocoa. Me dance it, yes. Me dance it to death. Every morning before me leave de house to go work, me rub me foot with wid de most sour lime you coulda find on de estate. A big dark green lime we used to call Maka-lemon.

Busha cocoa start to taste bitta. De merchant dem start to complain, say how de cocoa tasting "off". Me double de dose! Dis time dem say de cocoa really tasting bad. Busha strip all de trees. Say how is a fungus attacking dem. He give dem more manure. Me add worm oil to me foot massage! By the end of the six year

Busha lose every one of his customer dem an' de estate turn to rack an' ruin an' Busha get sick an' dead in no time at all.

An' dat is not all. In '38, just before de war, a white lady come from England — London to be exact — one Miss Bryden; say she is a close relative of Busha and she come with papers to see "bout de lan". She find me living by meself in de same shack dat Busha had give us but by den I had fix it up a bit. Well, she see "bout de lan" an' de man! She an' me strike up a relationship and, when she was leaving, she sell me a hundred an' fifty acres of some of de best lan on de estate for next to nothing. Plus she put another ten acres on it for free, as brawta, she say, for how me did mek she ... feel.

As time go by, me turn round an' sell most of the de lan' cheap-cheap to ex-workers of de estate. Dat is how dis likkle village start up here — Brydens. Me did want to change de name but it was there too long; it had stick in de people dem mind an' sometimes a mind is a hard fing to change. De night before de lady leave, we was lying down in de bed together and she say, "Alpheus, you know the main thing that attracted me to you when we first met?'"

Me say, "Yes." Because me done know de answer already.

She say, "What?"

Me say, "Me foot."

"Now 'ow would you know that?" she say.

Me say, "Is simple. Me is de Cocoa Dancer."

There was a long silence as he stared deep into his past, a smile of satisfaction playing on his lips. Then, as if noticing me for the first time, he turned in my direction and said, "And you are....?"

"Oh, f-forgive me," I stammered. "Anthony Bryden. From London."

(*2009*)

The River Flows On

No one knew the exact source of the river, but it started somewhere high up in the mountains and wended its way towards the east coast of the island, pausing to form a large pool somewhere in the Kalinago Territory before reaching the sea.

The Kalinago people used the river for everything. They drank from its clear water and used it for their cooking; they bathed in it, diving into its blue-green depths surfacing glistened, refreshed, reborn. But above all, they used it for washing and bleaching their clothes on the smooth grey boulders on its banks.

Lillian, for one, would never let a Monday pass without gathering all the dirty clothes, wrapping them into tight little bundles and, balancing the packed basin of clothes on her head, would make her way to the river. She was taller than most of the other women although she was only nineteen and she was by far slimmer. Her face was heart shaped with regular Kalinago features — her straight black hair cascading to her waist, contrasting with her parchment coloured skin. "*Ebè, mi yon bel fi*. What a pretty girl," the old men would say as she glided past them on her way to the river; "*Mounn nou bel, wi!*" Others would join in, "Yes, our people really beautiful, eh," and they would all nod their heads solemnly, earnestly wishing that they were forty years younger.

But suddenly a change came over Lillian. She would no longer go for moonlight walks with the others and at the river she would do all her washing, alone with her thoughts in a little corner of the pool, while the other women chatted a few yards away.

It was not her fault. Lillian had much to think about these days. She was in love. She had taken quite a long time to convince herself that she was, but now she was sure and therein lay her problem. The man she loved was Black and there was an unwritten law of her people that no Kalinago woman could have a Black man live with her on the Kalinago Territory.

She had first seen him at Marigot, a nearby village, while she was on her way to Roseau one Saturday morning. He came round the truck looking at the vegetables she was taking to market; suddenly, his gaze shifted from a bundle of dasheen, darted deep into her eyes, locked there and he seemed to be dazed for a few seconds. She did not see him again until two weeks later when he came up to the Territory in a jeep marked "Division of Agriculture". He seemed surprised to see Lillian there but he smiled broadly and began speaking to her. That is how it started.

She found out at that his name was Syd Joseph and that he worked in the Ministry of Agriculture in Roseau, but he was stationed in Marigot for the next six months. Soon, they were meeting regularly. She would have dinner early and ask her closest friend to come and look after her little siblings for her while she was out. Then she would run down to the smooth river pool, which was close to the main road and there Syd would be — waiting for her. He would use the government jeep to get there and they would spend the evening together with the music of the river in the background.

"This river ever change its course?" he asked her suddenly one night.

"No," she said, "Why should it?"

"Just for so," he said. "A change is always nice. A new scene to look at, a fresh angle on things". But Lillian was not interested in any deep discussion at the time. She snuggled up to him and fell asleep on his shoulder.

A few weeks later she realised she was pregnant. *Papa Bon Dyé!*

How was she going to tell her people, the Chief? She listened to the women gossiping loudly as they washed their clothes, telling the river all their secrets as she too had done. What was she going to do? She looked round and saw Ira's white teeth glistening against her black skin. She was the wife of Cor, the Chief's brother. Why could men have Black wives but the women not have Black husbands? After all, Syd was not even as dark as Ira, she tried to reason with herself as she prepared for the argument she was bound to soon have with the Chief. He would understand, she tried to convince herself. Everything would be alright.

That night she climbed the little hill and entered the Chief's two-storied house, the bright light of his gas lamps dazzling her eyes at first. The Chief had just finished his supper.

"*Wantwé, wantwé*, Lillian," he said in Kwéyol. "Come in." And they began making small talk on the usual topics; her family and the weather and the crops. Then she said suddenly, "Chief, there is a boy I love."

"True?" he exclaimed and broke into a fit of high-pitched laughter, his eyes turning into little watery black slits in his face.

She waited for him to stop laughing. Then she said, "He is Black." The smile faded from the Chief's face.

"No!"

"But I love him, Chief, and he loves me. And... and... I'm making a baby for him."

"No!!" the Chief said louder and she thought she saw a fire in his eyes. She trembled a little but she continued without pausing, speaking quickly. "He wants to marry me, Chief, and take me to live with him in Roseau. But I told him about my six little brothers and sisters and how Mama and Pappy died last year and I'm the only one who can help them now. He said that he would come and live here and he would show our people how to work the land and to make it give us more food that we can sell in Roseau to make more money and live better. He said that he would organise

13

the men into working teams and show them new ways to plant. And I would be his wife."

The tears were streaming down her face. The Chief was looking at her intently, his face stern and hard. There was silence as she looked at him, waiting for him to speak, but he just looked at her and thought and thought. Then he looked away and said, "I'll have to call the Council together to discuss it. They will come here tomorrow night and I will tell you their decision the day after."

The next night she met Syd by the river. They were both very quiet and just sat on the bank listening to the river babbling and laughing, as if it were laughing at them and their dreams. Then she said, "They discussing it tonight."

"Who?"

"The Council. They discussing if you can come or not Syd… They not going to let you come. I can feel it."

"Don't worry sweetheart. They must. After all, see how much I can offer your people. See how much I leaving for their sake. My home… my friends. And besides, it would be a waste if you would marry one of these men. They can not do nothing for you except to give you more babies. You young and you smart and you speaking English almost as good as me. With me you could become anything you put your mind to. I would help you. They must let me come, man."

These words comforted her a little and when they parted her heart was lighter. Syd said he would come up the next afternoon to see her land and plan where they would build a little house; he would also meet the Council and explain further his plans for the land. But all along the way home she could visualise the old men shaking their heads violently, stamping the floor and saying, "No! No!!" All of a sudden too, she remembered Justin, the Chief's cousin. She remembered that seven months ago the Chief had told her that Justin was in love with her and that he wanted to marry her soon. But she had taken little notice of him and especially during the last few months she had not remembered him at all…until tonight. Then she remembered Lizzie who had gone to live with her Black husband in Wesley, abandoning the precious, little plot of land she had owned. And then there was that horrible scene when Rita's Black boyfriend was found in her house one night and the Kalinago men ran him out of the Territory, stark naked as he was. She would never forget.

That night she hardly slept.

By the middle of the next day, the entire Territory knew the story. When Lillian went to fill her bucket in the river the women stayed away from her. She could see the children pointing at her, giggling and whispering to each other and the old men looked away as she passed.

Not a soul told her. But she knew. The Council had decided that Syd would not be welcome there. She hurried home and fell on the floor sobbing, her little brothers and sisters staring at her in wonder. They did not eat that day; she could not cook. And all afternoon she just sat in a corner and cried. Later however, she managed to go to the village shop where she would be sure to meet the Chief.

It was about five o'clock and the orange shades of late afternoon were dancing on the hillsides. Sure enough, the Chief was there and, as Lillian approached, the Council members gathered in a little group around him. A small crowd of people had gathered there also… as if to hear the sentence passed. But Lillian was determined to be brave. She held her head high and walked up to the Chief. Dead silence… except for the crying of a small baby. The Chief did not speak but slowly, shook his head negatively. Lillian let her head drop in defeat.

"I have arranged for Justin to take you and the child…." The Chief's sentence was interrupted by the sound of a jeep coming up the road. It stopped in front of the shop and Syd got out. He started walking towards the shop, smiling.

More silence. Syd stopped in his tracks. His smile died. The Kalinago crowd left the shop and advanced towards Syd forming a small semicircle in front of him. Syd took two steps back and waited. Then Lillian came forward, looked at him intently for a few seconds then put her head on his chest and let two tears fall, slowly, silently. Syd put his hand on her head and let it slide down her hair, passing over her shoulders and back until it stopped at her waist. Then he turned and walked back to the jeep, started it and drove off without looking back.

The crowd dispersed with a low murmur but Lillian stood there looking down the road and shouting to herself, "Syd! Syd!"

Presently, Justin stepped out of the shadows, took her by the wrist and led her back to his house on the other side of the river. To get there they walked on a line of stones laid out in the shallow water. As Lillian stepped on the last stone, her foot slipped and plunged into the cold river water. Shaking the water off her feet as she stepped on to the river bank, she mumbled under her breath, "One day that river bound to change its course."

But the river merely laughed and continued on its carefree way.

(*1968*)

Woman, Woman

This street is narrow and dirty, with stinking heaps of rubbish every few yards. It is crooked and unpaved, dusty in the heat of the day, and muddy in the wet of the rain. On either side, crooked and deformed little houses huddle close to each other, all dressed in the grey-black of rotten boards with dark brown hats of rotten unpainted galvanise enhanced only by the colourful sheets of tin advertising: "Breeze", "Du Maurier", and "Tide" that have been raided from the shop fronts to stop the holes at the sides of these shacks and to keep out the rain.

Slum. Slum so shameful that Morgan could hardly believe that he could walk down his dusty road and meet a wide smooth main road, just three hundred yards from his home. Then he could turn right on the road and reach the busy capital of the island with buildings almost as big as those he had seen in Florida when he had gone there as a fruit picker. Or he could turn left and reach the residential area, where the "rich folk" lived. That was where Mr Michael lived, Morgan's boss. And that was where Mr Michael's beautiful limousine stayed. Morgan was the chauffeur.

Chauffeur he was, but for how long? Morgan lay awake in the darkness of his hovel, unable to sleep. He knew he had been late for work four times last week, which meant that Mr Michael had reached work late. Last Thursday afternoon he had kept the car an extra hour after taking the children to school because hunger had forced him to search for something to eat. Mr Michael was vexed, he knew it. And it was all Iris' fault.

He turned over on his side; the light was getting stronger through the cracks in the closed window and the spaces in the partition. He could now distinguish the massive form of the woman sleeping heavily next to him. Iris. His wife. The wife who had given him their three little boys… all before their marriage two years ago. But it did not matter to him. They were legitimate now, nobody could call them bastard. And he felt proud as he looked at the three little bodies all crouched up on the rags on the floor at the side of the bed, their skinny, miserable dog, Poppy, lying across the legs of the eldest boy, all asleep.

Why was Iris trying to break up their little family? Morgan wondered. Life had already been so hard for them. He slapped a mosquito from his shoulder. In the past eight months he had changed jobs six times, and now that he had been able to scratch this job as a chauffeur to *the* Mr Michael, Financial Secretary of the island, she was trying to make things hard for him. He got out of bed, jumping over Iris in the process, and trying his best to be gentle so as not to wake up the others (and the people in the next room) with the squeaking of the bed. Iris moaned and turned over as Morgan opened the window with a screech from its hinges. The light blinded him for a moment; he did not know that it was that late. He went back to the bed and slipped on over his drawers the pair of long pants that was hanging there. The cold morning air over his bare chest made him shiver a little but he did not bother to put on a shirt.

He hated Sunday mornings anyway. Before, he always had them to himself; now he had to go to drive the Michael family to church. Every Sunday. But then, it was a way of life and he just had to do it. Besides, the pay was good. If Iris could have only understood that. Morgan went to the outhouse, lit the stove and put some water to warm for the coffee.

He was now getting twenty dollars a week, nine dollars more than he had received on any job for the last eight months. That was a fortune. At that rate he would soon be able to get out of these slums and go to live somewhere better, where the air was cleaner, fresher, freer.

He had only had the job for three weeks now, but he was determined that he was not going to lose it. From the first week he had decided that he was going to make an extra effort to be punctual. And he succeeded, right through that week; and he soon realised that he was in favour with the boss. This was his big break, the chance he had been waiting for. If he could improve himself; if he could create a good impression, then maybe he could even keep this job for a number of years… five, six years… he could even grow old being Mr Michael's chauffeur. And every year his salary would be increased. This was definitely the job he had been waiting for.

But then there was Iris. He had noticed those looks starting to come over her face the second week when he started asking for his breakfast earlier, his shirt starched and ironed, and when he brought home the new hat and tie. He expected trouble, and it did not take time to come. Last Monday she erupted.

"You has a nex' woman? You fink I donno? Nowadays you does want your food early-early so you can go by her before you does go to work. Nowadays is clean shirt, new tie, new hat. Sagaboy back in town! I know, oui. Is dat Diana you going back wif. Long before I did marry wif you, you used to run her. But if dat Diana believe dat she going an' take YOU from ME, she LIE. As I has a die to die she LIE."

Diana. Morgan smiled to himself as he took the hot water from the stove and poured it into two enamel cups with Nescafe. He had stopped seeing Diana a whole year before he had got married. He had forgotten about her; he was now a changed man. He had married Iris and was determined to make something decent of himself.

Morgan had not answered Iris then; he simply ate his breakfast

19

and hurried off. When he came in the evening he tried to explain the whole idea to her, why he wanted his meals earlier, the new clothes and so on… it was all for the job. But Iris merely said, "You fink you could fool me, eh?" and pouted for the rest of the week.

Every day was a repeat of the one before. Iris kept accusing Morgan of seeing Diana. What was more, she began using tactics: his breakfast was now late… and cold, she refused to wash, iron or starch a single piece of his clothes and on Thursday she refused to give him any food at all.

It was all these things that were affecting Morgan's job; and he was suffering it all peacefully, trying to keep his temper down for fear that if he did explode she would say that it was because her accusations were true. He suddenly remembered a verse he had learned long ago: "Woman, woman… what a blessing…" A blessing? He could not remember the rest but he knew it had to do with his situation.

He picked up the two cups of coffee and re-entered the room. He set down the cups on the windowsill and was about to shake Iris gently when he saw a mosquito sucking the blood from her arm. He raised his arm to slap it to its death in one mighty action, but he thought twice and caught his hand in mid-air. He brought it down slowly and brushed the insect away gently. Iris woke.

"Look you coffee, Iris."

Sitting up she took the cup from him and began to sip the hot coffee. "Wha's de time?" she asked.

"De church clock jus' ring haf pas' seven." He was unfolding the ironing board.

"It so late aready? Oh God, is time dose children wake up for dem to go to church." She proceeded to rouse the boys while Morgan crossed over to the outhouse and put two irons to heat on the stove. He came back to the room and sat on the floor resting his back against the partition. "Allan, Ken and Edward," he called to the boys. "Come and tell Daddy good morning."

The three little boys came one by one, hugged their father and then climbed on to various parts of his body. Morgan enjoyed this. Meanwhile their mother got a basin of water from the outhouse. "Come an' bade for all-you to go to church," she called out to the boys, "All-you will drink all-you tea after."

The boys were reluctant to go. "Go on," Morgan said and pushed them on gently. He crossed over to the outhouse and when he returned with the hot irons he took out a clean white shirt and began to iron it.

"Hey. Sagaboy pressing, Papa," Iris called from outside where she was bathing the boys. Morgan did not answer.

"Like Diana goin' an' feel fresh dis Sunday morning."

"Iris, for the last time, I has to carry Mr Michael to church dis morning, at nine o'clock. You doh fink I should try to look decent?"

"Look decent? An' last Sunday you did carry him in de same ol' clothes you did have the whole week, an' nobody doh say nofing. Why for you want to look decent so sudden like dat?"

"Iris, you make me late four times las' week aready, you doh fink I should try to do a little somefing extra for Mr Michael not to vex wif me so much?"

"I make you late las' week? If you stay too long by Diana before you go to work dat's not MY fault. All you men too bad, you hear."

Morgan could take it no more. He was going to provoke her, to look for a fight and give her some good blows. That would shut her up, and make her respect him. He said, "Well OK, so you know dat I does go by Diana. Well if so, dat's my own business an' it haven' got nofing to do wif you, you hear?"

"All-you hear him? All-you hear him?" Iris shouted in rage, suddenly becoming aware of the neighbours who were listening. She rushed into the room. "Is true, is true. You self say so now. I wasn' sure, but now you self say so."

Morgan turned round to answer Iris, but as he did so her clenched fist came down hard and heavy on his left eye. He raised his hand to return the blow, but he could not hit her. Her hand came down again on the same eye, harder than the first time. Blood. Now he did not know what he was doing. He made a mighty swing which spun Iris round and on to the ironing board which toppled to the floor with her. As this happened, one of the hot irons that were on the board slid down and collided with Iris' face. There was a terrible scream as the hot iron bit into her right cheek, transforming it into a little pillar of grey smoke that carried the scent of burnt flesh.

The neighbours rushed in from nowhere, the three boys began crying in unison and the air was filled with screams of various pitches as Morgan just sat, in a corner, dazed, until the ambulance came and carried Iris to the hospital.

He reached Mr Michael's home at quarter past nine, his left eye blue and swollen. Mr Michael, his wife and two children were waiting on the front step.

"Sir, I'm sorry. I'm…"

"Drunk again and fighting, and you come here and tell me that you're sorry you're late? Man you're not sorry. You're fired. Now get the car and take us to church as your last job."

Morgan thought of walking out, but he could not. He got in the car and took the family to church. He stayed outside during the service but he did not pray or think of God. He was only trying to figure out where his next job would come from and the bread and butter for his three boys and Iris. Iris? Oh woman, woman, he sighed.

When they had reached back home, Mr Michael paid him. "I didn't think you were the type," Mr. Michael said solemnly. "You disappointed me."

"Yes Sir," Morgan whispered. Then he took a long last look at the sleek shining car in the garage and began walking to the gate.

But Mrs Wallace, the cook, had seen the whole affair. She could not understand it and she could not contain her curiosity. She ran after him. "Morge, Morge, wait." Morgan turned around slowly.

"Morge, Morge," she said when she reached him, "What happen, nuh? Is somefing dat happen to make you lose dat job. Is somefing dat somebody do you?"

Morgan looked at her long and hard. Then shaking his head he said, "My own wife, Ma Wall, my own wife."

"Iris? Iris dat make you lose dis job?"

"Oh lord, yes, Ma Wall, is she, is she self," he said and he began to cry. He told Mrs Wallace the whole story unashamed of the flow of tears that was ruining his male dignity. "An' to see is we self I was trying to better, Ma Wall, we self. She kill our life, Ma Wall, mine, hers an' our free little boys, all kill."

"Doh worry", said Mrs Wallace, "I going to tell Mr Michael what happen, maybe he will take you back."

"You will do dat, Ma Wall? You fink he will take me back?"

"Maybe", said Mrs Wallace. "Now go home. Go an' see what happen to de little boys and Iris."

Mrs Wallace went back to her kitchen and Morgan started down the road. Iris? He said to himself, you fink I can go back to dat woman now? After all she do, after all she make me lose! Oh woman, woman. Then suddenly the whole thing came back to him. He stop dead.

Woman, Woman, what a blessing
We need them badly, I confessing
But at times dey does turn into terrible fings
Is dem we mus' fight back and prove we is kings.

Or something like that anyway. But it was true. It was what he had to do about Iris. Fight back. She just could not keep winning like that.

He began walking again. Towards a slum area. A slum area he had not been to for years. But he suddenly realised that he would have to ask somebody; he was shocked to find that he just could not remember in which house Diana lived. He searched about for a long time, but all in vain. Then he met a man who said, "Diana? Where you been, man? Diana gone to England four, five months ago."

Ah well, he would have to go back to Iris after all. Oh woman, woman....

(*1968*)

Cochie's Pwi-Pwi

All you haven't hear the news about Cochie, nuh? Well believe it or not, he building another pwi-pwi. Yes, it's true; I hear it from a good source, that Cochie building another pwi-pwi!! Well, well, well, this world have some people that mad, oui. From the time he had build the first pwi-pwi people had say that he was mad, but I had say, "No man, maybe the man was trying to help himself and things didn't turn out too right for him." But now that I hear that he building a second pwi-pwi I convince that he really mad.

Oh, all you don't know the business about the first pwi-pwi? Well let me give all-you the story. Boy that by itself is a joke.

Well, it was about 1954 or '55. I cannot remember too well, but anyway it was about the time when everybody was going to England. Cochie see everybody going to England so he decide that he going too. But poor fella, he didn't have no money, so Cochie decide that he going to build a big pwi-pwi and sail to England on it with his wife and two children!

The first person he tell about the plan was his wife Agnes herself. But although Agnes is a very foolish woman, when Cochie first tell her, she just laugh it off because she herself just couldn't believe that anybody could have a kind of stupid idea like that. But Cochie tell her that she could laugh as much as she want but he was serious and after four days of telling her about the plan Cochie finally convince his wife that what he was saying was not just a joke. When she realise that the man was really serious, she start to get real frighten.

"You don't know where England is, nuh?" she ask Cochie. And Cochie say, "Of course I know. England is somewhere up by Germany and Australia and those places." I don't know if Cochie had ever go to school, but if he did, he could never have learn geography, for the kinds of things he say.

Anyway his wife (she more stupid than him) say, "Right. And you expect to go there in a pwi-pwi?"

"But how you mean?" Cochie say, "You don't know that when Christopher Columbus leave England and come to the West Indies it was on a boat no bigger than the big pwi-pwi that he had come. Only to say that he had build a house on it, and had put a lot of pretty sails flying. But it was a pwi-pwi! And if Christopher Columbus could leave England and sail to the West Indies on a pwi-pwi, I don't see why I myself cannot leave the West Indies and sail to England on the same pwi-pwi?" And his wife didn't know what to answer and she could only say that she wasn't too sure that it was England Christopher Columbus had come from and in any case that was in olden days and times change.

Well, you know how Mahaut small; in less than no time, the whole village hear the rumour that Cochie coming down from the mountains dragging some big pieces of *bwa flo* and *bwa cano* behind him. And when they see that the rumour was true, they realise that the man was really serious and they have to do something about it. So a close friend of Cochie who they calling Big Ben (because he had go to England once and when he come back all he could tell them he see was Big Ben) decide that he going to talk to Cochie and try to make him see some reason.

Well, it was Wednesday night and at that time Cochie was working real hard on the pwi-pwi because he say that he must finish it for him to leave before the end of July before hurricane season start. So Cochie was working like the devil all day and at night he used to go by the rum shop to cool off his muscles and heat up his brain. On this particular night, Cochie wasn't drinking so much though; he was sitting in a dark corner listening to the other men talking about carnival and the days of *bann mauvais*. He was thinking how much he going and miss all that when he gone when somebody suddenly come up behind him and say, "Ay Cochie, how things coming, nuh man?" And Cochie turn round and squint his eyes in the darkness and make out that it was Big Ben. So they greet each other and start talking about all kind of things which Big Ben was only using as a warm up before he approach the real subject.

Well, at last Ben say, "But Cochie, I hear you going to England on a pwi-pwi you building. Is true nuh?"

Cochie say, "How you mean if is true? So you don't believe that a man could go to England on a pwi-pwi then?" And he give Ben the story about Christopher Columbus and his pwi-pwi.

Ben now don't want to get in no kind of argument with Cochie so he say, "Of course I believe a man could reach England on a pwi-pwi. But it would be dangerous. When I go to England we take ten days. Ten days on sea. And all you seeing for those ten days is just sea and sky. Garcon, I never know that the world had so much water!"

But Cochie tell him that that was when he, Ben, had go to England, but nowadays they have some boats that does reach in three days (I don't know where Cochie hear that). And the reason for that is because those boats know how to follow the "sea river".

Ben say, "The sea river? What is that? I never hear about that before."

And Cochie say, "Ah, you see? All you don't know nothing and all you want to talk." And he proceed to explain to Ben that the sea river was a kind of river that does flow in the sea starting somewhere in the West Indies and flowing straight to England. And all you had to do was to row far out enough and find the "river" and once you get in it you could just sit down and fold your arms and you going direct to England! That is exactly what

Cochie say, Big Ben himself, tell me so! So help me God, if I lie I die!!

But Ben himself did not know too much about what Cochie was telling him so he didn't know if to believe or not to believe; and he had really hear about different kinds of currents they have flowing in the sea — maybe this "sea river" was one of them. So he keep his mouth shut and he say, "But you sure you will find this "sea river" when you row out?"

"Of course I'll find it," Cochie say. "You forget I was a fisherman for ten years, nuh? I know all the rivers in the sea!" And there ended Big Ben's conversation with Cochie.

Well, Papa, the days pass, and in less than no time, Cochie finish the pwi-pwi and he call his wife Agnes to see it at the back of the house. I don't know exactly how big it was but from what I can gather it was big enough, maybe measuring something like ten feet by six feet and with two long oars on either side.

So when Agnes see it she say, "Bon Dieu, Cochie, it pretty eh? When we going?" Because by now Cochie had convince the poor woman that going to England on the pwi-pwi was as easy as going to Roseau on a truck. So he tell her, "Get yourself and the two children ready for next Sunday. And don't tell nobody, because I don't want a crowd!" And he himself start telling people that he wasn't leaving until the middle of August because it had come like a joke when people see him passing in the road to bawl out "Cochie, when you leaving on the pwi-pwi?" Most of the time he wouldn't answer, but now he start to tell them, and the whole of Mahaut start preparing to see Cochie leave in the middle of August.

But on the last Saturday in July, unknown to everybody else except his family, Cochie was preparing his things for he and his family to leave the next day.

Cochie start to load the pwi-pwi. And just hear what he put on it, nuh: two pounds of salt fish, a pound of smoke herring, a coal pot, a bag of coals and two kerosene tins of fresh water, plus a few pots, and cups, and so on. Then he get one of these big, big black umbrellas that had two patch in it already and he open it and nail it in a upright position in the centre of the pwi-pwi. Then he paint on it, big and bold in white paint, "S.O.S." because he had hear that was a good thing to have when you travelling — you could never lose.

So bright and early on the last Sunday in July, Cochie wake up his whole family and they all dress up in their best clothes and go to early mass; Cochie himself was wearing the big white suit you does always see him with on the best occasions. And direct after mass Cochie pull the pwi-pwi down to the sea — it wasn't far — and the whole family jump on board and they set sail. But not really sail, because he didn't have no sail and what Cochie really start doing was he start to row out. Well if it wasn't for one or two people who see them sailing out, nobody would have know that Cochie and them had leave. But those people who see them start running and calling other people to come and see and all those who could (some of them jump out of their bed) rush down by the sea in time to see Cochie and his family sailing for England on a pwi-pwi. I myself was there and I see them with my own two eyes.

Well, as the story goes, Cochie row from about eight o'clock that morning till about ten o'clock (that's what his wife say). Then he stop and he say he hungry. So he tell Agnes to start to cook the lunch. Come to light the coalpot now, it couldn't light. They had forget to bring kerosene to make the coals ketch. So Agnes start to cry, bawling how they would never reach England and how they would starve to death on the sea. Besides when she had start to see the water getting so deep and black underneath her she had really start to get frighten.

But Cochie tell her she too stupid and force all of them to eat raw salt fish and drink water telling them that the figs would ripen just now so them could eat them. Then Cochie start rowing again. But by three o'clock he get tired. He stop; and the sun was so hot that all four of them squeeze up under the umbrella and they go to sleep.

When they wake up — darkness. Agnes start to bawl again and the two children join her this time. Because all they hearing is sea doing "splataw…splataw" on the side of the pwi-pwi, and the wind blowing through the umbrella as if it want to throw it down. Well Cochie himself start to get frighten now and he pick up the oars and start to row and row, feeling that he was rowing in the direction of Portsmouth because he had know that Portsmouth was in the north so soon enough he would reach the sea river and life would be cool. But he row and he row until he get tired and he drop into a deep sleep again.

Well when they wake up the next morning they wasn't seeing no land at all — just sea and sky, but one thing they realise was that they were moving very fast and nobody was rowing. And Cochie jump up and start to shout, "We in the sea river. We in the sea river." And he start singing, "Arima tonight, Sande Grande tomorrow night" but he change the words to "Dominica tonight, we in England tomorrow night", and he make everybody sing and dance until they nearly capsize the pwi-pwi and they had to stop.

Everybody was happy, but not for long, because soon enough they realise that they had very little water left because they had drink too much the first day. So they eat the raw salt fish and smoke herring without no water and is then they start to feel thirsty and they drink off all the little water they had remaining.

Well Papa, the people drift for three days and they start to get weak and hungry and thirsty and thin. And Agnes start to sing *Libera* for herself and the others because she say that she was sure they would never see land again. And Cochie himself just lie down under the umbrella groaning and saying that England maybe move because they should have reach long ago.

But on the fourth day when day break, Cochie wake up all the others shouting, "Land ahoy! Land ahoy! We reach England." And when the others look they see some big mountains in front of them in the distance. But poor Cochie didn't realise that it was the same Dominica he was seeing and that he had only reach as far as Portsmouth.

And a white man who was staying at Morne Espanol happen to see this little thing on the horizon and he take a spying glass and he spy. And he see a big black umbrella floating on the sea with "S.O.S." mark on it. So when he see that he say that somebody must be in trouble, and he phone the police in Portsmouth to tell them about it.

Well, the Portsmouth police get a launch and they go out to see what was happening. And when Cochie see the police coming in the launch he start saying, "Look the England police coming to welcome us." And when the police reach and put himself and the others on the launch Cochie start shaking their hand saying, "Please to meet you. Please to meet you. I am one Angus Tamery from Mahaut, and these is my wife and children. We sail here all the way from Dominica, West Indies." But the police only burst out laughing and shaking their head and they tie Cochie's pwi-pwi to their launch and tow it back with them to use as evidence.

Poor Cochie! The tired he was tired and the hungry he was hungry and the hot the sun was so hot that it had fry his brains and the sea water he had drink the night before had make him so bazoodie that he had no idea where he was, who he was or what exactly was going on.

When they reach Portsmouth it had a whole crowd of people on the jetty waiting to see them land. And when Cochie land he start grinning and waving as if he was a king because he feel that was the first time somebody had reach England on a pwi-pwi. But when he was going to the police station (because that is where the police was taking him), he turn to the police who was holding him round his arm and say, "But officer, tell me nuh, how come England have so much black people? I thought it was a white man country."

And the police look at him and say, "England? Boy, you right here in the same Dominica you leave four days ago."

And when Cochie find out the truth they say he cry for three days straight. By that time the police had find out the story from the people in Mahaut, and a week later they put Cochie in prison because they say he nearly kill himself, plus his wife and children.

Anyway, when Cochie come out from prison he find his wife and children had go to Canada because Agnes sister had send for them. But Cochie behave very well although every day people troubling him saying, "Cochie, where the pwi-pwi?"

But lo and behold, look just yesterday I hear that Cochie building another pwi-pwi. This time is Canada he going for him to meet his wife and children. But he change his style. He say this time, he not following the sea river. His plan this time is to tie the pwi-pwi to the back of a banana boat and let it pull him to Canada!

Poor fella, I wonder what he going to do if he reach Martinique!

(1969)

Jonkunnu Story

Dawn does not break in this place. It cracks open, one zig at a time, each zag slightly longer than the other. Serpentine. Spewing a blue brown haze over the darkened landscape, masquerading as light. Nothing stirred as it crept up from behind Diablotin Mountain then slid down its western slopes in slow motion, coating the motionless skeletons of the hurricane-ravished trees with hints of green and the midnight purple of over-ripe star apples. Nothing moved when it stretched its long arms into the valley between the Pitons, feeling its way through the most intimate crevices of the low, spiky shrubbery, dipping its fingers in the night-chilled, dank waters of the sluggish stream that stagnated in silent pools reflecting what image they could muster of another day's dawning in Itiya.

The faded and mud-stained strips on Pitchie-Patchie's worn out costume barely trembled in the shadow of a breeze that had not the energy to lift a john crow's neck feather, that knew not where she had come from or where she was going, could not explain her own existence yet knew that she loved Pitchie-Patchie and all that he stood for. She called herself "Obilyere" for she thought perhaps she was the orphaned wind of some ancient storm that had crossed the land and left her there, forgotten. And so it was, through the gentleness of her heart she chose the defence of righteousness when the time came to choose.

She was the breeze that had once lifted Pitchie-Patchie's bright costume high into the sky so that he seemed to be ablaze with colour on the day he had confronted Horsehead in his claim to dictatorship and challenged him to battle. She was the same wind, strong and resolute then, that had caught Horsehead off balance and helped Pitchie-Patchie's rock-hard pouie stick to knock him over the lip of Cockpit Precipice and into the depths of Fond Diable. And she was the self-same reviving balm-yard breath that had cooled Pitchie-Patchie's fever and entered his lungs to make him live again when all of Jonkunnu-dom had given him up for dead. Now she looked at him with love and pity and pitied her own weak and debased condition. She knew that if she could only wake him from this bottomless sleep the island would have a chance to recover its identity, to take its place in the sun once more. And she knew that Pitchie-Patchie had the power within him to do it.

Why else would Horsehead have spent his last energies conjuring up his most potent biological weapons, which, in his bid to destroy one character, had sent an entire population into a deathlike sleep that was now in its thirteenth year?

The denizens of the neighbouring islands of Xaymaca and Acinimad had gaped at their television sets in horror that night as they watched aerial shots of Itiya darkening and shrivelling before their very eyes. First the leaves had turned brown and dried up; then, as they began to fall, a frantic wind dashed about trying to gather them to herself while making futile attempts to place them back on the withering branches. Stems, which by then had darkened, twisted into contorted figures such as had never been seen before in this part of the planet. Next, the shrubs and grasses darkened, and froze into cardboard like versions of that stiff and spiky leaf known in some parts as mother-in-law tongue. And they too broke off and rolled along the barren land in great rustling balls of decaying compost that the mothering wind tried to harness and keep in safe places should the need ever come to replant the earth when this dry, dark season was over.

34

Then a great silence came over the land as Pitchie-Patchie fell first, since he was the main target, then Belly Woman and Policeman, Jack-in-the-Green, and the Red and Blue Set girls. Next fell Wild Indian and Sailor followed by Jaw-Bone, the House Jonkunnu and finally Koo-Koo, the Actor Boy, who through his training had been able to maintain an appearance of wakefulness longer than anyone else in that ill-fated country.

Now, thirteen dark years later, the remnants of Obilyere circled helplessly, uncertain what to do. If she could only gather enough strength to wake Pitchie-Patchie, the island would stand a chance. But how was she to do that when she knew that she was barely a breeze now and Pitchie-Patchie was deep in a sleep of the seventh degree? And Horsehead, with the help of Devil and Cowhead, had been able to crawl out of Fond Diable and unleash his tyranny on the sleeping island. What could a feeble rebel wind do?

She had lingered there, believing that one day she could literally be the wind of change that would resurrect Itiya and its near-dead citizens. But she could also feel that time was running out; she could feel the life draining from her tired arms, could see that she was but a dying breeze. In the darkness of that morning's dawn, she knew that she had to act now or accept defeat and fall asleep along with Pitchie-Patchie and the band of peaceful Jonkunnus.

The little wind took in a deep breath, then released a burst of energy that sent her spinning in a full circle, clockwise, then another and another, until she was rotating at a terrifying speed; faster and faster, stronger and stronger. Then when she knew that she had the power to make it, she changed direction and swooped down towards the land. She headed for Pitchie-Patchie, who was lying there, half-buried in the mud in the half-light of that fateful day.

High on the pinnacle of Mount Diablotin, Horsehead shifted uneasily. As usual he had slept badly and despite all Devil's reassuring and Cowhead's low moaning, which was intended to soothe, he could not help feeling that something was amiss. At five thirty in the fore-day morning, he raised himself from the large clump of dried razor grass that he called a throne and a bed, dragged himself to the shaggy edge of the mountain top plateau and switched on the laser beam of his searchlight.

The flowered print on the neck cloth that elevated his head several feet into the air was faded, worn thin and ragged from his frightful battles with Pitchie-Patchie long ago. It gave him little protection from the cold mountain air so the dry teeth in the dry jawbone of the dry horse skull of his head chattered like the pebbles in the tin shaker of a jawbone scratch band in Belize or Tortola. He steadied the pebbles with one hand and used the other to hold an ancient telescope to the black hole of his dry skull that was his eye.

How had it come to this sorry state of affairs, he asked himself, as the lasers panned the plains and valleys below searching for a sign of life, the slightest movement that would betray a would-be insurgent. Of late he had been growing weary of being despot of this sleeping island with these two imbeciles, Devil and Cowhead, bowing and scraping before him, but planning, he was sure, to make a shroud of his neck cloth the first chance they got.

No one could be trusted these days, not even those you protected, and had removed from their debased conditions and turned into princes, albeit, of Darkness. He longed for the old days when he and Pitchie-Patchie were the kings of Jonkunnu-dom, when their colours were bright and vibrant and the Blue and Red Set Girls competed with each other for the privilege of dancing at their sides during the Christmas parade.

Not even Jack-in-the-Green or Koo-Koo, the Actor Boy, had a patch on them when the fife and the drum got fired up and transported them way back to the time before time in the motherland when they could possess the bodies of the ancestors and enjoy short glimpses of what it was like to be human.

He remembered, too, the long and painful journey across the vast ocean, with the wailing and gnashing of teeth seeping from deep within the belly of the sailboat that thrashed below them for three endless long months. Then finally their arrival in these islands of the Antilles, beautiful beyond words, but deadly and full of the suffering in the belly of the boat. But such had become the way of life the ancestors bore with as much dignity as they could muster. And so it was that once a year, at the festival called Christmas, they were called out to show themselves for two brief days, too brief to sustain an existence.

It had been Pitchie-Patchie, Horsehead remembered, who had been the first to recognise that they were a dying breed. And when he suggested that they make their own life on the plains and valleys of Itiya, a small hitherto uninhabited island between Xaymaca and Acinimad, all Jonkunnus applauded loudly. "And like the fools we all were, agreed to make him our leader." Horsehead sighed loudly and laid the telescope aside for a moment, to think about that auspicious day when they had all arrived at Itiya with their costumes glowing in the midday sun. Mirrors and brass buttons flashed in their eyes, drums and fife kicking up a storm like they had never heard before. What a glorious day it had seemed.

What a glorious, disastrous, completely doom filled day it was when that bundle of rags became our leader.

I didn't choose what had to be done... I let fate run its course. So here I am today. Ruler of a peaceful sleeping country. Crime statistics non-existent — not a murder or break in or rape, or even the slightest altercation, in thirteen years.

But damn! How I miss the sun and the rain, the green of the forest, the blue of the sea and sky, the sound of the river and waterfall, the birds, and, especially those butterfly days when the pale yellow *amoris filadelfi* hatched and fluttered through the sky in long undulating lines before gathering in their thousands to make love to the purple flowers of the lignum vitae like a burst of daytime fireworks round the heads of the trees.

Oh the thought of it! Oh the sheer joy of the sight! This dark, listless, lifeless, sleeping, nothing-happening, boring existence must end! "Me cayn tek it no more," he cried out, which awakened Cowhead, who sprang up from a deep sleep and looked round in a daze.

"Get back to sleep, you pitiful inaccurate imitation of a female bovine," Horsehead snapped at Cowhead, and Cowhead, accustomed, as she was now, to Horsehead's increasingly sour moods and uncalled for insults, rolled over once, snorted twice, and dropped back asleep.

Horsehead returned the telescope to his hollow eye, switching off the laser as by now the blue-grey light of the non-day had started its deepest descent down the western slopes of Mount Diablotin. He let the telescope lead him from south to north along the rugged coast that had once been a silvery white sand beach. Now the land was nothing but a stretch of dry mud, edged by the sea and browned by the silt of a sluggish river, that vomited its foul waste at various points along the coast, creating a grey froth that surrounded the island like a flotilla of alien canoes that lacked the inclination to go anywhere.

He knew that somewhere on that beach or near the river's slimy estuary Pitchie-Patchie lay asleep. If only he could remember the exact location, if only he could assure himself that nothing had changed, that his enemy was at bay — literally. If only...

In his anxiety, Horsehead scanned the shoreline and the land but forgot to make his customary survey of the skyline above the dry trees, just on the off chance that one day an attack could catch him off-guard from the skies. In fact, had he looked, there was no guarantee that he would have been prepared to meet what he saw. Thankfully, as it turned out, he confined his gaze to the desolate coastlines trying with all his might to remember where last he had seen the heap of mud and rags that was the sleeping Pitchie-Patchie.

Pitchie-Patchie, Police, Sailor, Jack-in-the-Green and Actor Boy sat high in the branches of a clump of leafless forest at the foot of Mount Diablotin's northern slope. They dared not move a muscle or utter a word as they had seen Horsehead's laser scanning the island, and they remembered that the enemy's survey usually lasted a good hour or more before eye strain would set in and Horsehead would throw himself down on his razor grass throne, where he would thrash about in frustration and self pity, before falling asleep again.

Two hours later, Pitchie-Patchie felt it was safe to talk. He kept his voice low and gentle but loud enough for all to hear, even Horsehead. And despite the seriousness of what he had to say, it still carried that hint of laughter that came so easily to him.

"My friends," he began, "this morning we were all awakened by a gentle breeze that came from I-don't-know-where to bring us back into the real world. It seemed like I was asleep for just a few hours, but a check on my pocket organiser shows that we have been asleep for thirteen years, four months, two weeks, five days, twenty-two minutes, and fourteen seconds. I take it that you all can remember how we arrived at this condition…"

"Can't remember a thing," said Jack-in-the-Green. "It all just seems like a long nightmare."

"The facts are simple," Police said. "Pitchie-Patchie led us to this island so we could survive in a land of our own and have an existence without having to depend on humans to provide an occasion that allows us to manifest."

"In fact, these occasions were becoming so rare that we were on the point of extinction," interjected Koo-Koo, the Actor Boy.

"Exactly," continued Police. "Apart from the efforts of a few well-thinking humans with above average intelligence, we were as good as dead. Then old P-P here got this idea that we might stand a chance if we could create a life of our own, if we could have a land of our own. A land where no one lives but us."

"Itiya."

"Exactly. Itiya. A paradise on earth for self-indulgent spirits like ourselves, lying in the middle of the Caribbean and waiting to materialise. It was so perfect, it was such a brilliant idea that we decided to make Pitchie-Patchie our leader."

"And Horsehead didn't like it."

"Exactly."

"And challenged Pitchie to a one-on-one fight for supremacy."

"Worse than that. He threatened to destroy Itiya if he was not accepted as ruler."

"Seems to me like he damn near succeeded too."

After a moment's hesitation, Pitchie-Patchie also found a rock to use as a pedestal; but he looked on the crowd with pity and tenderness. "Who will lead them if I don't?" he asked himself. "And if another leader should appear, where will he lead them?" He had no answers, but ventured to speak first. He raised his hand and the crowd fell silent.

"Horsehead," he said. "Many are the years we have spent together and many are the hours I have sought your company, taking your advice and listening to your words of wisdom. We have spoken and acted together like brothers for five centuries or more, always with the intention of achieving the best for our people. What madness was it therefore that overtook us thirteen years ago when we split our oneness in two and brought this tragedy upon ourselves, our people and our chosen land. This is not what we had planned. This is not what we wanted for ourselves or for our country.

"These thirteen years of my sleep have been filled with only dreams of a new tomorrow, unity and understanding returning to this island. In my youth, I was under the misconception that the greatest role anyone could ever play was to rule. Now that I am full of thirteen years of dreams, I have discovered that our greatest calling is in fact to serve. I wish no longer to oppose you, I bear you no hatred, jealousy or malice. Instead I want you to know that I love you with the same love I hold for every Jonkunnu that ever was and ever will be.

"I can now only ask you to accept that love, accept our allegiance and remove your obeah from the face of this land and let it be green again, let it rain again, let our rivers flow again, let our sea and sky be blue again, let the sun shine again, let our hearts and faces feel joy again. But above all, let there be butterfly days again, when the pale yellow *amoris filadelfi* hatched and fluttered through the sky in long undulating lines before gathering in their thousands to make love to the purple flowers of the lignum vitae like a burst of daytime fireworks round the heads of the laughing trees."

There was a long silence before Horsehead replied.

"My brother, I cannot. The obeah was stronger than me or you, much stronger than I imagined. Thanks to your efforts the island still exists, albeit in this state of near death. Were it not for you and those who helped you it would have been completely destroyed and none of us would be standing here today. You were able to lessen the impact, but look at what it has caused.

"I acknowledge the folly of my ways; I really meant you and our people no harm. I have had thirteen long years of sleeplessness to reflect on all this and have come to the same conclusion that you have reached in your sleep: that it is more honourable to serve than to lead. But then there must be leaders as there must be followers. It is the law of nature and no country can prosper without both. The greatest achievement that can ever be attained therefore is to be the Servant-Leader.

"It is now given to you, my brother, to prove that this is true and possible. Take up the mantle of leadership of our land. I too am old and tired and have no more interest in the affairs of state. I bow to your greater wisdom, I dedicate my life to your leadership."

And a great cry rose up among the Jonkunnus and many of them ran up to Pitchie-Patchie saying, "What kind of land is this he is now handing over to you. And why now? For thirteen years he has kept us asleep and not once tried to wake us. Let us not accept his offer. Let us fly from this island and find a new land of our own. Let us leave him and his two accomplices alone to rule over this dark and desolate place."

But Pitchie-Patchie would have none of it and said, "This land is our own. It may be dry and empty and desolate now but let us not forget the days when it was good to us, gave us sustenance and brought great joy to our hearts. I cannot turn my back on this land any more than I can turn my back on you or my brother, Horsehead. All Jonkunnus were spawned from the same great imagination of the ancestors and our future cannot be fragmented in small pieces scattered across the face of the earth."

Then after a long pause, taking a deep breath he said, "Horsehead, I accept your offer and your love." And some say that when they moved towards each other to seal their agreement with an embrace, they saw a teardrop sparkle deep inside the hollow of Horsehead's eye.

"Come," Pitchie-Patchie then said to the dumbstruck crowd of Jonkunnus, "We shall all live on the mountain top. From there we will certainly see far better just how we can save this land and ourselves for the generations to come."

And as they began their trek towards the mountain top a joyous stream of fresh water came rushing over the cliff as a waterfall and down the river bed, bright green leaves sprang from the dry tree branches, the dark clouds over the island began to shift and give way to clear blue skies. All over the island Obilyere began a dance of joy, carrying in her arms long undulating lines of yellow butterflies that fluttered through the sky before gathering in their thousands to make love to the purple flowers of lignum vitae like a burst of daytime fireworks round the heads of the laughing trees.

(2011)

Lizards Don't Lie

Jan was certain that a large, gray lizard had followed her out of Ikal's house in August Town and had jumped onto the roof of her white Lada station wagon as she sped out of the yard leaving a cloud of dust that paled the red, green and gold of the front door and the crowd of neighbours jostling for a look at her lover's body lying in a pool of blood on their bedroom floor.

She had heard the heavy thump of the croaker as it slipped in through the back window but she had refused to look. She could feel its gloating presence as she raced past the University Hospital and squealed round the corner near Papine market. She could almost see it tighten its grip on the seat back as she swerved to avoid a bikeman who darted in front of her from Papine Square heading down Old Hope Road. Because he seemed vaguely familiar, she challenged him to a race down to Liguanea. He was fast but she stayed with him as he danced deftly among the lines of traffic, slipping through the narrowest of spaces, swaying gracefully from side to side, his head encased in a black helmet that glistened in the ten o'clock morning sun, a few locks escaping down his back, his shirt billowing like a flag behind him, a long object wrapped in scandal bags attached to the side of the bike.

She was certain that the lizard had dropped to the floor when the lights at Hope Pastures turned red and she screeched to a halt. The bikeman went through. Damn him. She would get him yet. But he was nowhere to be seen in Liguanea, or in Half-Way Tree, not on Eastwood Park or on Red Hills Road. By the time she turned into Havendale he was out of her thoughts and visions of Ikal's head in a pool of blood came swarming back, each larger, stronger than the former, more vivid, more painful than the last. She needed some space, some air, someone to talk to. Perhaps Greg and Pat were still home…

She parked in front of the house she had once shared with Greg and Pat, and entered quickly through the dark garage. But the croaker followed her in. She could sense it sliding between the discarded boxes and rusty barrels. As she went into the kitchen she could hear it scurrying among the unwashed pots and glasses on the counter. She knew that it had walked upside down on the ceiling as she passed through the corridor into the living room and out to the back porch where it slowly crept down the wall and settled over her left shoulder as she sank gratefully into the cushions of a large wicker chair that faced Red Hills and the cool breezes that blew in from them. She inhaled deeply, taking in a scent that was so sweetly familiar, then exhaled loudly, put her hand on her forehead and closed her eyes.

"So it take this to bring you back here, eh?" It was Swithen. He was standing in the doorway leading to the living room, his head cocked to a side, droplets of water hanging from his locks fresh from the shower.

"If you want me to leave, just say so, awright. Me didn't come here to look no argument."

"No argument at all," he said holding up his hands in surrender. "Just want to know what I could really do for you… under the circumstances."

"I just need a friend to talk to. I thought Pat or Greg would be here."

He chuckled, getting the point. "They left before me get the news."

"Who told you?"

"A friend. You know how news travel fast." Then after a pause. "Jan, you know I'm here for you… in spite of everything." Jan said nothing.

"You know how I felt about you and Ikal, but this…"

"You don't have to apologise, Swithen." He paused, then said, "Me hear the medic dem say him was killed since nine thirty last night."

She opened her mouth to say that that wasn't possible. That she and Ikal had made incredible love at day break. But she closed her mouth and said nothing.

"So that make sense to you?"

"The medics got it wrong. Ikal was alive when I left for work at five o'clock. Ras Jerry saw him go jogging at six. He usually gets back by seven. It would have had to happen after that."

She had called Ikal just before six soon after she had passed the tollgate on the Millennium Highway, heading to her office in Mandeville, the cool morning air kissing her face like another lover. She got his voicemail. "This is Ras Jerry answering for Ras Ikal. Him can't talk now. Him cyan talk at all. Leave a message. Him will get it."

"Hi, Mister lover, lover. Just checking to see if you alright. Seem like me nearly make you sing this morning. We do it like that every day me will mek you talk in no time, mark me words. Me love you. Will wait for your call."

Ikal usually called her at six thirty and would tap the phone twice to let her know it was him. That way she would let him know that she had arrived safely. But when she got to Mandeville he still hadn't called. She sensed that something was wrong. She called Ras Jerry who lived nearby. Jerry said that he had seen Ikal go jogging at about five thirty but had not seen him come back.

"Go check him for me, noh," she asked Jerry.

Jerry called back twenty minutes later to say that he had found the door open, entered the house and discovered a narrow stream of blood across the bedroom floor that had led to Ikal's body under the bed, his head bashed in at the back.

"Or so Jerry say," Swithen said after Jan had recounted the sequence of events.

"Is him call the police."

"What them say?"

"Nothing. Ask me a set a question as soon as I reach, that's all."

"Bout what?"

"How long me there with Ikal. What time me last see him alive…"

"So…"

"Wha'?"

"When last …?"

"Is wha? You's a police too?"

Swithen paused and looked at her. The lizard cocked its head to look at him.

"You know there's a big rasshole lizard just above your head right now?" Swithen asked.

"Yes."

"Wha' happen? You 'fraid lizard?" She knew that Swithen was terrified of lizards. They made his skin crawl. On looking at this one now a slight shudder ran through his shoulders, which he tried to suppress.

"When you gwaan grow up, eh?" she mocked.

Swithen stared hard at her, remembering when they had first met and become friends, their early happiness, their alienation once she had met Ikal, how he could no longer stand the sight of her… how he still wanted her. He kissed his teeth, gave a little laugh and walked away, shaking the water from his locks, letting them tumble down his back like a river in spate.

A hot rush of blood ran through Jan's body and her stomach turned over. Lawd, she thought, 'im favour Ikal down to the walk an' all. And he knew it. He turned to look at her and flashed a grin as he entered the living room. She got up and followed him inside, something going soft inside her, in spite of herself.

He turned to face her. "Look, you can rest up here for as long as you like. And don't worry. Me nah go trouble you. In fact me soon leave."

Jan's tears didn't fall until Swithen had left the house and she was back on the porch with a glass of juice and the photo album she had left on the shelf under the TV. "Pictures will do it every time," she whispered as she gazed at the first few with herself and Ikal. They were of their first outing together, a hike up to Blue Mountain Peak with her gym gang. She had met him just six weeks before at the Institute of Business Management where they were in the same MBA class. He had caught her eye on the first day of class and a few days later when he stayed back to transfer some notes onto his laptop she went over to him. He was bent over his work, his locks hanging down the sides of his face like a curtain.

"Hello Mr Diligent," she said, "Look like you plan to mash down this course." He looked up to reveal the most perfect teeth in the easiest smile she had ever seen.

He said nothing.

"Wha' happen?" she continued, "Cat got your tongue?" He shook his head then motioned with his hands pointing first to his mouth then motioning "no" with his hand.

"Oh, you're..." He nodded.

"But you can hear."

"Perfectly," he signed. She smiled. He smiled bigger.

In a month they were lovers. Not a sound escaped his lips; not a grunt or a howl or a scream could he make, this silent lover. But sometimes she could swear that she heard the tiniest little squeak from the depths of his throat as he climaxed. She took this as a sign of hope that one day he would make a sound, say a word, speak a sentence. I'll make you sing yet before me done wid you, me lover-lover. Just you wait.

She had noticed a drastic change of attitude in Swithen once he realised what was going on. "So what a dumb Rasta can do for you?" he asked her in the middle of a game of Kalooki soon after. The question had come as a surprise to her. But she was cool. She laughed.

"Him just nice, you see. Just irie. Me love him too bad."

"And me, now?"

"Swithen, man, you is me bredren. Me love you dat way. Everything irie, man." She laughed and rubbed her hand over his scalp-low hair cut.

It was soon after that he started growing his locks. Jan noticed and smiled but said nothing.

"So is what de bredda trying?" Ras Jerry asked one day when he, Ikal and Jan were driving in the hills above Kingston. "Him feel him coulda ever look like you Ikal?"

Ras Jerry had become Ikal's self-appointed voice ever since their school days. A Bobo Rasta now, he wore a khaki turban and carried a staff with lions carved along its shaft and at the head, made of solid silver, he said, the shape of a hand holding an egg delicately between the thumb and forefinger, symbolising the frailty of life and sovereignty, from the kingdom of Abomey.

Ikal looked at Jan for her response. "Swithen is me bredren, Ikal. It has never gone beyond that. It never will."

Ikal nodded, pulling Jan to him and kissing her on her forehead.

"Me too," said Ras Jerry.

A year later Swithen's locks were as long as Ikal's. And he had started to smoke ganja.

"Ikal don't smoke ganja you know," Jan said to him when she found him sucking on a huge spliff on the back porch one lazy Saturday afternoon.

"And 'im call 'imself a Rasta?"

49

"Is not all Rasta smoke ganja," Jan retorted.

"Den all dem so is not true Rasta and is unworthy of the locks pon dem head and is a disgrace to His Imperial Majesty." Jan knew that she couldn't reason with him.

She kissed her teeth, got into her Lada and drove to Mandeville. She had got a job as assistant manager at a new hotel there, which meant leaving for work at five in the morning every other day. That could be hard, especially when she was in rehearsal with the University Singers. But the only thing she loved more than the choir was Ikal. And now that Swithen had started smoking ganja she felt that the time had come for her to move out… and move in with Ikal. She would discuss it with Ikal that weekend.

But when the weekend came she was having second thoughts, which flooded her mind as she drove into Kingston that Friday afternoon. The four of them in that house were like family. Even Swithen, with all his recent stupidness, had really been like a brother to her. She worried about him. She wondered if he was already beyond ganja. They all had reputations and jobs to protect.

As she drove into her driveway she decided she would discuss it with Greg and Pat that night, then with Ikal the next day. If everything was alright she would move the following weekend. She parked the car and entered the house through the garage, as usual.

"You reach home well early today." It was Swithen, standing in the doorway leading from the kitchen to the living room. "What happen? They fire you for smelling of ganja or what?"

She ignored that. "Can I please pass?"

He paused a while and then moved his body slightly to a side. As she passed he leaned forward so that he rubbed hard against her body. She smelt the ganja on his breath. He followed her to her room.

"So if you find me so disgusting why you rubbing me up so?" he asked mockingly.

"I don't find you disgusting, Swithen," she said as she put her bags on the bed and began unpacking them. "I find you, childish and petty. You're bigger than that, man. Don't act so small."

"So wha'? You find this small?" Jan immediately knew she was in trouble. She turned round slowly to look at him. Swithen had unbuttoned his pants at the waist to reveal the bulge in his underpants.

"Swithen, please don't do anything stupid now. I beg you."

"Stupid? You think you and me making love is stupid?" He advanced on her. She backed away.

"Come Jan," he said. "You know you want it." He leapt at her grabbing her by the arm. She pulled away trying to get to the door. He threw himself at her.

"No Swithen! Swithen nooooo!!!" She screamed as she remembered what she had been taught many years ago by a friend. She raised her knee violently upwards and caught him hard between the legs. His mouth opened in a silent scream, he doubled over and crumpled to the floor like a rag, holding his stomach and moving his mouth in a mime of agony that Jan could only imagine. She grabbed her car keys, dashed to her car and drove to Hellshire, where she sat on the beach and cried her heart out.

Two hours later she called Pat. Both she and Greg were home now. Swithen wasn't in. She drove home and told them what had happened. Then they drove to Ikal's house and told him what had happened. She swore she would never go back to the house once Swithen was still there.

A month later Swithen called her. Said he wanted to apologise. Didn't know what he was doing. Must have been the ganja or something. Jan almost said that it must have been the 'something' because ganja don't mek nobody act so, but she stopped herself.

"It's alright Swithen," she said. "I forgive you. We can put the incident behind us and carry on as if it never happened."

A few weeks later she was shopping at Hi-Lo in Barbican when she felt a presence behind her. She looked round to find Swithen standing there. She stopped.

"Wha' pen, Swithen," she said, "so you stalking me now or what?"

He laughed. "Nothing like that, man. Just wanted to say hello and see how you doing."

"I'm going just great. How 'bout you?" He fell in next to her as she walked the aisle selecting items carefully from the shelves.

"Me? Me's awright, man. Decide to clean up me act. Stop smoke, so no more ganja smell pon me. Bet cha me smell nicer dan de one Ikal now," he teased.

Jan laughed. "Swithen, Ikal wash 'im locks in hibiscus leaves every weekend and mek me rub him down with musk oil every night after 'im shower. The last ting him do before him go to bed is chew mint leaf. I think you would have a ways to go before you could get to smell dat good. But I glad to hear you coming back to yourself. You could really achieve plenty if you only give yourself a chance."

"Maybe if I had a good woman like you by my side me would do better."

"Plenty others better dan me out there, sah. Just tek time and look well."

"Jan, I..."

"No Swithen. Enough. We done talk already so just lef it nuh. Look, I have to run." She literally ran to catch a cashier with no line.

"Run all you want," he snarled. "You must come back one day. You mark my words."

She rushed out of the shopping centre, leaving him standing in the aisle like a jilted bridegroom.

Living with Ikal came easily to her. She soon felt like this was where she had always lived. Always would. The neighbourhood embraced her as she embraced it, knew all the children's names, made small talk with the old folks, fed their chickens her leftovers.

The only thing that troubled her at first was the lizards. But even that she got used to. She decided that she wouldn't let them spoil her newfound happiness. And when she noticed how cool Ikal was with them, how he smiled at them and joked about how much they said that they liked her, she stopped worrying about them completely.

Now on the back porch she stared at the one that had followed her here. She wondered if he knew that Ikal was gone, if he knew who had done it, if he had followed her here because he too needed a friend. She fell asleep with him there, a single tear still creeping down her cheek.

The sound of Greg's car in the driveway woke her up two hours later. She sat up as he and Pat came to her. Greg held her hand.

"We just came from the house," Greg said. "Police still there. Ask us a whole set of questions."

"Like what?" Jan asked.

"If you smoke or have lapses of memory; if you always talk the truth," Pat said.

"Really? Why?"

"Well," Greg continued, "the medics said that Ikal was killed at about 9.30 last night but you told them that he was alive when you left for Mandeville at 5.30 this morning."

"That's true."

"You sure?" Greg asked.

"Greg. When I left this morning Ikal was sleeping on the bed, breathing heavy, lying on his side with the sheet pulled up to his neck. They found him under the bed, Greg, under the bed. With a major gash at the back of his head as if he had been hit from behind. You think that all that could have happened with me lying next to him asleep?!"

"You had spoken to him when you got home last night?"

"The rehearsal had gone on late. He was sleeping and I didn't want to wake him."

"And this morning when you left…?"

"I got up, showered, got dressed and left."

"How you know if there was no blood under the locks?"

"Greg, up to now there is no blood on the bed. Besides…" She stopped.

"Besides what?"

She didn't answer. Pat put her arm around her. "It's alright," she said. "You don't have to say any more, Jan. We understand."

"Besides…" Jan said, "… We had just made love."

The scene came rushing back to her. The alarm on her cell phone had gone off at four thirty as usual and she was dragging herself out of bed when suddenly a hand reached out and caressed her back. What a man love sex, she said to herself and smiled. She slipped off her nightie and lay back down in the bed. No morning light was breaking through as yet. The room was pitch black.

Immediately his hands were flowing over her, smoothing her shoulders, her neck, her stomach. She could smell the mint on his breath, feel his heart pounding against her thigh, her face, her navel, touching her like never before, taking her to a new place of intense pleasure. In no time she climaxed in an explosion of ecstasy that reminded her of their very first time together, that sent her gasping in ecstasy and kept her there for several minutes. When she came to, Ikal was getting on top of her. "Wait, Ikal," she said. "You forgetting the condom. Easy, easy." She reached for the drawer in the bedside table, took out a condom and put it on him. His lovemaking became more intense than she ever knew. He erupted in an orgasmic frenzy and yes, a sound came from his mouth. A sort of scream that, in its strangeness, could have been one of extreme pleasure or absolute terror.

"Ikal you did it!" she said in a whispered shout. "You made a sound! That means you can do it again! You can learn to talk, Ikal! You can learn to talk!!"

But he was too exhausted to celebrate anything at that moment. Soon his breathing was slowing down and he was falling asleep. So she just lay there next to him enjoying the moment until she suddenly remembered what time it was, dashed to the shower, dressed and sped off to Mandeville…with a smile on her face.

"What you smiling at?" Greg now asked.

"Memories… just memories," Jan said blissfully. She glanced up at the ceiling to see if the lizard was still there. He had moved from the corner and a little towards the centre of the room, almost directly over her head.

"Rahtid," Pat shouted when she saw what it was Jan was smiling at. She jumped up from the couch and ran to the entrance of the living room. "Jan move. Suppose 'im jump pon you."

"Dis lizard never trouble a soul yet," she said. "Is me frien." Pat kept her distance.

"Me cyan stand dem tings," she said. "Dem love to jump pon people."

"Lizard know who fi jump pon," Jan said. They all looked up at the lizard in silence.

"Chaw! Leave him be," Greg said after a while. "Him soon gwaan." Then he continued, "Tell me something Jan. When you reach home last night you went in the kitchen?"

"Went to the fridge and poured a glass of water."

"And you never notice anything unusual."

"No. Why?"

"The police say that Ikal was killed in the kitchen and then dragged under the bed."

"Dem still trying to say dat Ikal was dead when I reach home?"

"The doctor who examine the body…"

"Dat doctor don't know a dyam ting. I tell you Ikal was alive when I leave home dis morning. We made love. I see him. Ras Jerry see him."

"And Jerry see him come back?"

"No. Don't think so. I don't know. He seemed a bit confused this morning, maybe from the shock. Besides seems him lose this fancy African staff that him always have. But Jerry wouldn't lie. He an Ikal is bredren from long. 'Im used to talk for Ikal, you know, explain to people what Ikal was saying. Until me start to be deh wid Ikal."

"An Ikal used to pay him for this work?"

"Me don't know if you could call it pay. 'Im used to give him 'a smalls' from time to time."

"Until you arrived on the scene."

"Well…yeah."

"I see…"

There was a long pause. The lizard took three steps forward and swung his tail to the right.

"So," Greg continued, "this Ras Jerry enters the house and just goes straight under the bed to find Ikal lying there dead."

"Lawd Greg! You is worse dan a police. You lose you vocation, man. You should be working for the CIA."

"Or could be a lawyer," added Pat.

"Hey. Enough the two of ounu. Answer my question, Jan."

"Im di adore Ikal like a king. 'Im coulda never do something like that."

"So how do you explain this?"

They spun around. It was Swithen. He was standing on the little patch of lawn in front of the porch holding a long object wrapped in black and red scandal bags.

"What's that?" Greg asked.

Swithen did not answer. He looked at them for a minute then pulled a blue handkerchief with paisley design from his back pocket. He carefully untied the string that held the plastic bags around the object and, using the handkerchief to hold it, he held up Ras Jerry's ceremonial staff. The top, with the silver hand holding an egg delicately between thumb and forefinger symbolising the fragility of life and sovereignty, was covered with dried blood.

"Where you get dat, Swithen?" Jan hissed.

"Went round Ikal house after the police and everybody leave," he said. "Thought I would do some investigation of my own."

"Lawd, dis house full of detective," Pat mocked.

"Me find it not three chains from the house, in the rubbish heap in the gully."

Jan was not convinced. "We cannot just assume anything," she said. "We don't know how this happened. I told you Ras Jerry told me that he couldn't find his staff this morning."

"Oh come on Jan. You're not going to fall for that story," said Swithen.

"How about your story? Where's your proof?"

"There must be finger prints. I was careful not to disturb them."

"Let's call the police," Greg said, heading inside to the phone near the TV. "Come Swithen, you have to talk to them."

"My pleasure," Swithen said and stepped forward. On setting his foot onto the porch, the lizard cocked his head, took aim and shoot himself through the air at lightning speed, spreading front and back legs like wings and holding his tail stiff behind him, he landed directly on Swithen's cheek and clung there. Swithen let out the strangest sound, a scream that did not want to be heard, half choked half released, the indistinguishable holler between pleasure and pain that confuses the world and brings it tumbling around us as its truth is revealed.

Jan froze and stared at Swithen in disbelief. She recognised the scream. She had heard it in the darkness of Ikal's bed that morning. Then, she had taken it as a song of hope. Now it was a knoll of condemnation. Swithen who was frantically ripping the lizard from his face and dashing it to its death against the wall suddenly stopped when he realised what had happened, his breath coming in short hard gasps as he stared back at Jan.

"Jan." She heard Greg calling her from the living room, his voice sounding far, far away. "The Inspector say he want to speak to you first."

But she was unable to move. Her eyes locked hard with Swithen's.

"Jan! You coming?"

"Yes, Greg, I'm coming." She finally managed to say.

She got up and moved towards the living room. But on reaching the door she stopped and looked back at Swithen again. He was standing there with his back to the hills holding Ras Jerry's staff and looking so much like Ikal. And as a wind blew in from the mountainside she was sure she smelt the fragrance of hibiscus leaves and musk and mint.

(2006)

The Man Who Loved Clocks

For as long as anyone could remember the old man fixed clocks. He had a dark and cluttered workshop in the cellar of his house on Bath Road and there he kept every shape and model and type of clock you could imagine. There were large wall clocks and small bedside clocks, pendulum clocks and weight oscillation clocks; clocks that were wound up with large black keys in three places on the face and clocks which were wound up in two places in the back; clocks which chimed and clocks which alarmed, plain old geezers and gay young buzzers, tickers and clickers and cluckers and plodders and even a stern old grandfather clock and a gaily painted cuckoo clock, both so rare on the island then. There was a funny little Swiss clock with a wooden boy and girl who twirled onto a little veranda each midday and midnight to dance out the hour. The old man had been given it by a German lady who had lived on the island for many years but had gone back home to die. And there was an elaborately carved baroque clock with cherubim and seraphim and clouds and garlands that surrounded the face so completely that it was impossible to tell the time without feeling that you were staring through the gates of eternity — in which case time wouldn't really matter anymore. That one had been brought in for repair by a Frenchman from Martinique who said that it had belonged to his grandfather who had taken it with him from St Pierre a few days before the 1902 eruption. It had been repaired but no one had ever returned for it, and the Frenchman had sailed away many years ago. Yes, interesting and important clocks lined the dark shelves of the workshop — all covered with dust and some with faces so dirty that you could hardly discern the fading numerals. But all — every one of them — working.

You could descend into that cellar and swear that you had gone down into the engine room of some vast vessel that sailed the sea of time — indeed, which kept time itself moving — the burring cogged wheels and the whizzing hair springs and the ticking and the tocking and the starting and stopping of hammers and escape mechanisms and main springs was such that one always had an instinctive desire to speak as loudly as possible without shouting over them in the hope of not being outdone by the clocks — although that really wasn't necessary.

Except, of course on the hour, when every clock which had a voice would raise it to high heaven and belt out an anthem to time which could be heard for several blocks and which could last for ten minutes or more depending on the hour and due to the fact that some clocks were slower than others. To the astonished visitor it would be the most incredible sound — but for the old man it held no particular significance and he would just keep right on working through the performance only stopping to listen from time to time if he picked out from within the cacophony, some new chime of a recently repaired piece that now formed part of this time-shaking chorus. And then he would smile.

He was a kind and simple soul really, whose wife had died some years before. It was said that he had children who lived in New York and London and who by then must have been themselves old, so long they had departed. He had few friends and fewer enemies if any and so, apart from his clocks, he gave some attention to his cat which slept on the shelves among the clocks and through their chiming without the opening of even one eye to acknowledge the sonorous hours. And in every room of the house above the cellar, he kept a clock — a chimer too — so the chiming passed from the basement of the house to the uppermost ceiling in one continuous flow and the entire house was consumed with the time and the chimes of the passing hours.

His personal timepiece was a pocket watch with a long thick chain of solid gold which he kept in a lower pocket of the faded waistcoat he always wore. It had come from Cayenne and was a gift from his wife one Christmas. Before she died he had promised her he would wear it always and in truth he treasured the watch like his life.

But there was one more mighty clock in town which the old man loved and revered above the rest. It was the cathedral clock which sat on the central steeple of that self-important building which stood proudly on a rise of ground in the centre of town — the largest and tallest building for miles around. And for chimes it had giant bells that were triggered by a series of ropes and levers connected to the massive wheels and cogs of this authoritative clock which controlled the very life of the little community. The dong of its bells sailed out from the belfry in strong sure waves that spread over the town, and inside the houses, up into the central valley and over the wooded hillsides that overlooked the little capital on north and south. Its bells announced christenings and first communions, confirmations and feast days; they peeled at weddings and tolled at funerals, dictating the mood of the townsfolk. Out to sea they went and woke the fishermen in their boats, sent children scurrying to the bathroom for morning school, rang them out for midday lunch hour and ended the workday with the ringing of the Angelus at six in the evening. At Christmas it fixed the exact time of the birth of the Saviour, at Easter it then hailed the risen Christ and it, and it alone, it seemed, had the authority to end one year and usher in the next with twelve solemn and officious strokes.

How the old man wished to own that clock, to be part of it and to care for it. It had a power over time and life which he longed to possess and since it had been installed by a Belgian priest many years before anyone could remember, it seemed to go on untended except for the church gardener who pulled one of its ropes twenty times to wind it up once each week. It had a mystical life of its own, a life force, concluded the old man, which it had received as a special gift from God Himself. It was God's clock which He used to control time and life of the island, if not the world. And to think that he could be part of this plan, this divine scheme of things if only... if only.

But the clock went on and on with never a sign of fatigue or wear.

The old man took to going for walks around town on Sunday afternoons; down the main street onto the Bay Front, along the sea and up the little hill to the church where he would stand and stare at the divine clock and wait for six o'clock to strike so that he could synchronise his own watch, holding it out at arm's length, the long gold chain swinging from his belly like a strange umbilical cord.

And as he got older and less healthy, he was still watching time pass on that relentless clock.

Then one day it happened. The church clock stopped. No one knew how or why or what exactly had gone wrong or what to do. But it had stopped and a fair amount of confusion reigned in the town as could be expected, that first morning without the clock. "Send for the old man on Bath Road," said the Father Superior. "The one who fixes clocks. Surely he can get it going again."

"But he is old and sickly, and very weak these days," answered the young priest who was in charge of the cathedral. "I doubt very much that he will be able to go into the belfry and climb the ladder into the loft and fix the clock... but we can try him anyway."

When the gardener brought the message to the old man, he found him lying in bed in his dark bedroom breathing heavily because the pains came harshly across his chest now and he found relief only by lying quietly on his left side.

"The church clock stopped?" he asked, sitting up slowly on the side of the bed. "But it can't. It's not possible."

"It stop this morning at five past two," said the gardener. "The hands still at that same time up to now. The priest ask you to come fix it."

These last words rang like a bell in the old man's ears. If he was feeling weak and feeble a moment ago, here was strength; if he was choking earlier, here was breath; if he was dying earlier that morning, here now was life. Here at last was his chance to control time and life along with God and he was not going to pass up on it. "Help me get dressed," he said to the gardener, "I'll come with you."

The first flight of steps, through the choir balcony and into the belfry was not so hard. He took it slowly, the young priest in front, the gardener behind, their footsteps echoing loudly in the empty church in the still of the day. He had never entered the loft before and he was filled with an awesome sensation of wonder and privilege to be doing so.

He looked up and saw the young priest climbing the ladder above him, his white cassock flaring out like a woman's dress around him, mimicking the look of the giant bells as they climbed past them. It wasn't a tall ladder but it suddenly seemed like it was disappearing into the clouds and the great clock of heaven would be hard to find among them. He felt himself sway a little.

"You sure you can make it?" he heard the gardener say from below him.

"Yes…yes, j-just hold me at the back of my leg as we go up," he answered.

When he emerged, head first through the square hole in the floor and into the loft the silence was even more deafening. The light streamed in through the three windows in the front of the steeple and looking over the shoulders of the statues, three saints that stood like guardians of the mighty clock, he could see the silent town below him, brilliant in the morning sunshine, as if waiting on his mechanical skills, to come to life again.

The gardener breathed heavily behind him. The young priest's cassock shone white against the background of the sea and the town outside, and so strong was the glare of light from behind his head that the old man could not see his face or discern his features.

"Well," he said. "Can you fix it?"

The old man looked across the narrow room and beheld the massive machinery of God's great clock. Giant wheels and main springs and counterpoint balances like he had never seen before, huge hammers, and stoppers and ropes and pulleys that descended to the enormous bells that bellowed through several holes in the floor. It was large and confusing and totally unexpected.

Panic suddenly seized him. He would not be able to do it. He had been presumptuous, he knew, to dare to think that he and God could run this clock together. This was God's great test and he was failing. He did not know where to start or where to look or what to move. He felt a cold sweat break out over his body, the pain shot across his chest and he jerked forward slightly to receive it. The clock works merged into a single mosaic of ropes and machinery and he felt himself falling.

He shut his eyes and saw it all clearly — his very life depended on it. If he could not get the clock going again and soon, his life would end there in the loft, and he would have failed to answer God's great offer to run the world with Him.

He opened his eyes again and then he saw it: a thin chain about two feet long dangling above a giant hair spring. With automatic lucidity, despite his growing shortness of breath, he realised that the chain had broken from the end of the spring causing it to redouble upon itself and unable to accept the momentum that would be generated by the winding effect of the ropes. The chain should be re-attached to the spring but now in its broken state it was too short.

His hand shook. His vision blurred again momentarily. Slowly he reached down into his waistcoat pocket and pulled out his pocket watch. The long gold chain dangled from it. From his tool bag he used his pliers to detach the chain from the watch, and with wire and clippers replaced the broken chain with his own gold watch chain, fastening one end to the coil spring and the other to the beam above.

"Go downstairs and pull the wind-up rope right down," he told the gardener, sweat streaming from his face. The gardener obeyed. The coil spring curled and tightened into itself. The old man moved shakily to the large pendulum that hung in front of the machinery, and swung it.

The clock came alive.

His breathing became even. His chest pain disappeared. He went to a small clock face that controlled the hands of the mammoth one outside and looking at his watch, he put God's clock on time.

Then walking past the young priest and onto the window sill and between the statues of the three saints who guarded God's clock, with a little laugh, he stepped out into the dazzling bright sunshine, onto a passing cloud and sailed away into the clear, blue sky.

(*2003*)

Parting

I've always known this, but I know it better now — parties are a place to meet interesting people. Even when it ain't carnival, parties are a kind of masquerade.

A few months ago, in Trinidad, a man from Dominica went to stay with friends who took him to a party on a hill because they thought he needed cheering up. He was a tall man, with short hair along his graying temples, and his white shirt, which was open at the collar, had pyjama cuffs, which stated softly that perhaps he was an artist who had known some success.

The drive was long, and on the way he smoked in silence in the back of the dark car, compulsively adjusting rimless glasses, which were tucked high on his nose. Every now and then he would hunch with his elbows on his knees, remain so for a while, then fall back into a slouch with his arms stretched out along the leather top of the wide backseat, a Newport twitching in the corner of his mouth.

He was new to smoking and didn't quite know how to hold a cigarette, and with unmoving brows he tried to recollect how he had directed actors to puff with confidence on stage, trying different grips as he thought. Every grip was followed by a drag and every drag was followed by a cough. Every now and then he would nod toward the eyes that watched him in the rearview mirror. Sometimes he'd hold them in a stare, sometimes he would drop his head in his hands or raise it up and keep it there like he could see right through the roof.

The smoke had caused the coughing, he was willing to accept. But not the smoke just by itself. The air-conditioning. Pelham's sport cologne. The musk oil streaked on Tina's neck. The showroom odour of the new Accord.

At the sprawling house, which was perched on a ridge near the foot of Fort George, he quickly accepted the invitation for a tour. The host was a middle-aged Indian who had made his fortune selling textbooks, and he gestured broadly as he spoke above the volume of the music, which vibrated through the walls.

"So how you know Pelham and Tina?" the owner asked, while the coughing smoker gazed blankly at the front of the house, which was three stories tall and made of concrete and cut stone. They were standing on the lawn, and the owner was again relating that the stained-glass trim on the windows and doors had come from an old train station in Leeds. When the station was razed, his son who worked there as an architect had bought the precious glass "cheap, cheap, cheap" and shipped it to him in a forty-foot container, each piece carefully wrapped and tucked in among the various household things.

"So how I know Pelham and Tina?" the coughing smoker paraphrased. He rocked back and forth in the damp grass, looked up at the star-spangled sky, and paused to watch the gyrating mass of bodies on the deck of a projecting section of the second floor.

"They said you were staying with them," said the owner, whose name was Anil.

The coughing smoker grunted, "through work", but stopped short of explaining that he was a banker like Pelham though he had also worked in theatre since he was a child. What would have been the point? Anil was a bookseller whose big new house had only one shelf of books. On another evening, at another time, he would have said something snide. But to be snide you have to feel superior, and in this case he did not. The man had things he didn't have.

The man had his son.

"I got the glass because I wanted to give the house a spiritual feel," said Anil. "Like a temple or a church, you know. The way they kidnapping people in Trinidad these days, in all you do, you better keep God close by."

"God does whatever he wants to do," the coughing smoker said, taking a pull and coughing through the menthol-scented smoke. Under his breath, he said, "If he exists at all."

He glanced up out of habit when he said this and shifted to the side. His reaction made him feel stupid. His shift had been reflexive, but in any case too slow, nothing you could say was lightning quick, nothing that could beat a thunderbolt. So what had been the point? There was no point. Which was the point. Which was why he felt stupid. Stupid in the presence of Anil whom he thought of as a stupid man.

Self-conscious now, he began to see himself the way that others saw him, and saw himself the way he was — terse in speech, erect in posture, shoulders square, gaze slanted — and he made a show of moving like the music moved him. It was a fast, percussive soca tune, repetitive and simple as rain, but he moved slowly, torso bouncing on the baseline, head nodding off the beat.

"This is a good fete you have here, my friend… nice house too… but by the way, you heard anybody say if they found a chain?"

"No. You lose one?"

"I think so. The clasp was giving trouble and I forgot to fix it." He slipped his hand inside his shirt and made quick searching moves along his neck. "Listen. I catch you later. I going and retrace my steps."

He lied. He hadn't worn a chain in his life. Yes, he lied. And so have I… but not directly… in a way. You could call it acting. I'm a coughing smoker. This is all about me.

Tina met me in the living room, which was overdone with stuffed chairs in frames of dark wood. In another house, mahogany is wood you would assume, but Anil is the kind of guy who had imported dark wood from Botswana at four times the cost, who had make a point to buy things that allow him to say, "Is one in the island. Only one in the place."

Tina sat across from me beneath a heavy chandelier. There was a glass table between us and we made small talk. She used to be a flight attendant and she had read some news in the *Guardian* that morning about BWIA that made her think for sure that by year end the airline would be closing down.

She asked about Anil and I answered while imagining whole scenes in which he appeared with his son, the son telling him that it was insensitive and plain stupid to have a contractor redo the plans he took the time to draw, and him telling the son that he think he know every damn thing because he go to big school in England. Line by line, beat by beat, scene by scene, I built it up, while Tina in a low red top and tight black pants, hair pulled back in a frizzy bun watched me through the mentholated haze, bemused. In another country, Tina would have been mistaken for a trophy wife. She was thin with high cheekbones and breasts that were pert even though they had nursed four children. With a shade seen only on brass instruments and certain roasted nuts, her skin was a lust-arousing bronze.

"There's a fellow been asking for you," she said. "Say he wanted to meet you but kinda shy. Say he writes plays and he did you in CXC. You want me bring him to meet you?" Before I could reply, she added, "I going to find him and two glass o' rum."

I was expecting a boy of eighteen or so, but instead I met a man. He was dark with a nose that looked like a frog about to jump; and without looking I could tell his skin was rolly-rolly where his head met his neck.

"Roger John," he said to introduce himself, while swiftly executing several moves — taking my hand, lighting a cigar, sitting down, and shaking his head as he cleared his throat.

"Lemme tell you something," he began, in a voice whose loudness I was sure would get no less if the music was turned down. "You change my life and you don't even know. If it wasn't for you, I would still be doing what I was doing before. But because o' you I leave that one time. I was a police. From I leave secondary school I gone in the force. And I moving up and moving up and moving up and t'ing, getting promote and promote and promote, but I never feel no satisfaction. And I keep saying, 'Is what so? Is why I ain't satisfy?' Same time, all my friends and them was telling me I had a flair. Cause I is a man could take off anybody from I was a small, small child. Any little t'ing you could say or do, I could do it just so."

He held out the cigar to me as if it was a ganja spliff. I reached for it and then declined, remembering that when he spoke he made a kind of squashing sound as if his mouth had extra spit.

"So anyway," he continued, "I say maybe is because I never pass no subjects in school. And I start to study that, and when they kick me off the force cause they say I taking bribe and all kinda mix-up, Anil hire me as a bodyguard, cause you know dem fellas and dem like to kidnap dem Indians cause they have the money to pay. So one day, he ask me where I get my flair and I say I have that flair from I born and he now tell me that I belong in show business. And you know what? Is like God was talking to me. And I say I going and develop my talent. But I say at my age now I ain't want to start at the bottom so I say lemme take some evening classes and do some subjects. And when I doing English Literature I come across your play, *Uncle Tom Never Come Back*, and I say, 'You know what, boy, you should stop this foolishness 'bout show business and all that, but you should still use your natural flair — cause I'm a people person — and write some plays.' So I start to write some skits. Well, as you know, Anil is a businessman, and when I show him what I doing and tell him that

I ain't bothering with the classes again, he say this t'ing could make some money, and he lend me some and I put on the play and it was a hit. And the rest, as they say, is luxury. You ever hear 'bout we? Crack Up & Company."

The look on my face must have told him that I hadn't, so he went on talking and I leaned forward with my elbows on my knees as if in deep interest, but the truth was that I'd seen a woman who even in this country could have been a trophy wife, and leaning forward offered me a better look. She had come around and down the spiral stairs behind and to the right of him, paused to look into her bag, then moved toward my right, his left, drawing my eyes and not my head, in sly pursuit.

When she disappeared out of the living room into the passageway, I felt compelled to cast my mind around the corner, to pursue a glimpse of her through concrete walls. In those days, I was no longer what you would call a believer. I had already lost religious faith; but I still had trust in certain instincts, still believed I had the knack for telling when a special thing would come my way. My wife, Maria, used to call my instincts *animalistic*, used to cuss and say I was a ruthless predator who needed flesh to stay alive, that my instincts had one purpose, finding women dumb enough to stray 'way from their herd. Yes, I've failed Maria. But she's not the only one. I've failed more important people in more fundamental ways.

"Roger," I muttered, as I thought of one of them, "Can you bring another rum?" He had begun to talk about collaborating on "a modern type o' version" of *The Joker of Seville*. He continued slinging words across his shoulder as he walked away. When he reached the landing of the spiral stairs, I turned my head to watch the wall.

My palms began to itch and I rubbed them as I talked to Maria in my mind — I've never found seduction easy. It's never really simple. At first. There's a part in the beginning when the glands are warming up and the old fears about yourself are hard and cold. When the glands are warm and the fears heat up, the fears will melt. But till then they're hard. Like rock. And you think you'll never be able to lift them up or roll them back or mash them down.

If you back out soon, you can be safe. But if you stick it out, man, if you stick it out, and the glands warm up and their heat begins to cause the fears to melt, you'll get a high, a real high, and you'll feel like you can play any role you want, that you can play the man you used to be, the one with the prospects, the good playwright, the good husband, the great father — no the great dad — and you'll feel a jet of coolness just below the surface of your boiling blood.

I was in the middle of these thoughts when I sensed the woman coming down the hall. The music was too loud for me to hear her steps along the marble floor, so I stood and looked at Anil's art collection, which was not as bad as one would be inclined to think. With my back toward her when she came into the room, I thought, I would sweep around and catch her from a turn. But as I timed her, voices shot above the music like a flock of startled birds.

"Come here, girl, and meet me father." I heard the woman laugh and suck her teeth, then Roger asking, "You deaf or you dotish or what?"

The woman sucked her teeth again.

"Come," he said, laughing. "Come. This man is me father right here."

He caught me by the arm and turned me, used his other hand, the one with the rum, to fan the woman over, then he gave me the glass. He was standing to the side. She and I were face to face. She was as dark as dried blood, with a plump upper lip, and she wore a floral dress with darts that made it fit. Above her low neckline there was a heavy line of shadow where her bosom pressed together, and a fading scar beneath her right collarbone.

The first words I heard from her were: "Lord, Roger, why you like to misbehave so?" The second set of words were: "Nice to meet you, Daddy, but I have to run."

I was in the back yard when I saw her again. Two hours or so had passed. There were three retaining walls that kept the house from sliding off the ridge into flickering Port of Spain, and I was sitting on the highest one. Light was spilling from the house and draining down towards me, streaming in between the trees, beading on the blades of shaggy grass. My mind was heavy and the weight of all my thoughts had drawn my chin towards my chest. My eyes were closed. I felt sleepy. Five rums had passed and I was trailing off.

I was halfway gone when my nerves began to buzz. There was a drone inside my head — a slur of heartbeat, music, tree frogs, crickets, wind, and distant human voices, plus the intermittent murmur of an engine woken up to take some people home — and something had disturbed it. Before I looked, I caught her smell. It was musk so I expected Tina. I don't remember how I felt when I saw her.

"Is OK for me to pass?" she asked from twenty feet away. She had the wariness of someone speaking to the owner of a cranky-looking dog. "You OK?"

"Yes," I said, still sitting. "Yes. What about you?"

"I didn't mean to dis you like that before, but I had to take care of a little thing."

"Oh. Don't worry. I didn't take it too badly."

She crossed her arms and moved towards me. In her heels she was a little tentative, and every time she lost her balance she would make a squeaky sound. But soon she was in front of me, so close that touching her would not involve the full extension of my arm.

"You not from Trinidad…" she began. Now my senses were fully aroused.

"Dominica," I said coolly. "But I live in Jamaica… Kingston, Jamaica… where the bad-johns live."

"I couldn't catch the accent. But anyway…" She began to say something, then changed her mind and tried to make a clever observation: "Everybody nowadays is a mix-up, they say."

"So they say."

"I gone for a smoke." She picked her way along the wall some yards away and lit up. "Don't mind me," she said when I caught the early whiffs of ganja. "I could move further down." She was making a bit of a fuss about bothering me, but it was clear she wanted to talk. When she's good and ready, she'll come, I thought. She's what? Forty? Forty-five? A little younger than me. We ain't no students. Either of us could teach this class.

Up the slope in a diagonal, two shadows came from two opposite directions, looked around, then lay down quickly in a chaise besides the pool.

"The smoke is OK?" she asked after being silent for a while.

"Come here often?" I replied without looking. I lit a cigarette. But before I could insert it, I began to cough.

"Not really," she said, coming over. "But I had to come. You know how sometimes you run from something, but as time goes on you realise you can't run anymore? How sometimes you try and resist something and you try and try until you give in because you face the fact that you can't resist anymore? Well, is like that. I had to come out here. I have a thing to do."

"Anil is your boss too?" I said, pretending to be naïve. "Not just Roger John's? Big party going on and the man giving you things to do?"

"I never said anything about anybody," she said, shifting her weight from one leg to the next. "Is more like I'm on a sort of mission."

"Oh, excuse me," I said in Roger's voice. "Lemme turn my back. Imagine, such a big house with so much space but not enough bathrooms to handle a normal fete crowd. Dem people is crosses in truth."

"With such a serious face, who woulda think you was so dotish?" she said through a chuckle, as she put one foot up on the wall right next to me.

"If you on a mission," I said, "who send you?" I was thinking that I knew these kinds of games enough to know that all we had to do was keep it going till one person dropped the subtext and came out straight. Directness would be the cue to act surprised, then flattered, then confused.

"Who sent me?" she asked, slowly bending and straightening her leg, like she was warming up. I brushed imaginary dust from her pumps. "Yeah. Who sent you out here at this time of night in a place where it have bad-johns who live in Jamaica? Where they ain't no decent men? Only rogues."

"Your son."

"Roger is a fella full o' jokes, eh? You know he's not my son, right?" I began to explain, then changed my mind. What would have been the point? The whole thing was too silly. Too complicated. She must have known his introduction was a joke.

She began to answer, then cut herself off. Fell silent. It was an active silence, one that kept demanding that we talk. I wanted to talk — for there to be talking. Talking had lifted my mood. I didn't quite know what to say. I was in that stage before the glands had fully warmed, and the old fears were still looking heavy and tough. I began to smoke again.

If either of us had walked away at this point, there'd be no story to tell. But maybe it wasn't just the staying. Maybe it was the staying plus the cough. Because it was the cough that made her touch me. It was a simple pat on the back, then a resting palm, fingers kneading knots from my shoulder.

Without asking, I laid my face on her raised leg. The skin was warm and damp with perspiration and must have been smooth. I don't know. I'd planned to wait awhile before I rubbed.

"You know, I'm not here to talk about Roger," she said, holding the weight of my head with the muscles of her thigh.

"I know," I said, my mind advancing to the moment when she'd let me touch her in more daring ways. I wrapped one arm around her calf and drew it closer. She pulled away, dropped her foot, and took some hasty backward steps. "I was sent here by your son."

I picked up my rum glass, which had been sitting on the wall. I shook my head and drained the glass. "You wouldn't understand."

"How you so sure?"

I passed the glass from hand to hand. "Because… Because… Because there are a lot of things you don't understand."

"I might surprise you."

I wheeled around and threw the glass away. "My blasted son is dead."

"My blasted son is dead." I'd never said it that way before. I'd said that he'd passed on, or made his transition, or gone to a better place, but I'd never said he was dead. Death is something for old people, something appropriately final for people who've gotten to a certain age, something as wide and deep as the sea at the end of a long highway. Young people aren't made for death. Death doesn't suit them. Doesn't fit them right. They haven't lived enough to earn their eulogies. They haven't paid the price.

Since Pierre's death six months before, I'd been trying to pay his debt, been trying to lead a better life. Trying to make it so that when my time came I'd earn the eulogy for both of us, trying to make it so that when they spoke of me they'd talk about how much I'd changed because of him, how much I'd used my life to live his dreams. Pierre was a dreamer. He wanted to do everything… make music, make movies, make art… make me understand that he was not going to be a replica of me… make peace with me, make peace with himself, with his sexuality, make sense of what it meant to have attention deficit disorder… make sense of a world that refused to remain in one spot so he could focus. Could take his time and look.

When he said he thought he'd do better in college somewhere else, was I too glad to pay the fare? Should I have kept him there in Kingston, the place that my career had made my home, to watch him suffer, watch him lock himself inside his room, watch his pants drop down when he didn't eat for days? Should I have encouraged him to try another treatment, get other drugs prescribed? Was it too easy to say yes when he said he'd like to go? Was I really trying to help him or help myself? Was I right or wrong?

"My blasted son is dead," I said again.

"I know," she said, and crossed her arms. "I know."

I needed comfort. Badly. I asked, "What's your name by the way?"

"Chloe." She came forward once again.

"How are you, Chloe?"

"I'm OK."

"I'm Irving, by the way."

"Nice to meet you."

"So," I said, "how do you know about my son?" His death was small news even in Toronto, so I figured she'd heard about it from Pelham or Tina. People see. People ask. People talk. Chloe could have asked them what was wrong with me, why I seemed so down, and they could have said, *Poor thing, he lost his son.* But instead of being reassuring, her *I know I know* felt glib. Pretentious. Airy-fairy cryptic. Which made me feel toyed with. Irritated. Annoyed.

"I know things," she said. I shoved a cigarette in my mouth. My hand was trembling. I couldn't light it. She reached to help me and I slapped her hand away. The cigarette fell. I stomped on it. Kicked what was left of it. Raised grass and dirt in the air.

"When I was fifteen," she said, while backing off, "I was living in Blanchisseuse and I caught a fever and started to burn. It took three days before my mother realised that I was really sick, that this was no ordinary thing like she was telling the neighbours for two days. By the time she could get some men to put me in a van and carry me to the clinic, they said I was dead. No pulse. No breath. When they got to the clinic, they put me in a room to wait for the doctor to come and pronounce me. But everybody knew I was dead. When the doctor came he gave me a shot and told the nurse to give me some chicken soup when I woke. She looked at him like he was crazy and he said a single word — 'typhoid' — before explaining that although my vital signs were very weak, I wasn't gone. That is one death. My second death was fifteen years ago. I was working as a junior secretary in the Red House when Abu Bakr and the Jamaat stormed the place and held the government hostage. That was 1990 during the coup. They shot several people. You remember that? Well, I was one of them."

She moved toward me now with her arms crossed and went to sit again where she'd sat when she'd begun to smoke her spliff, and I walked over. She wiped her face and said, "No," as I approached, and it was only then that I saw her tears.

"Both times," she said softly, as her shoulders squeezed up, "my soul looked down on my body from above. I saw it all. The nurse in the country clinic. The surgeon in the theatre down at General, searching for the bullets in my chest."

Lightning looks for water. Men are drawn to women's tears. If I dig deep enough to analyse it, I might find out why. Maybe it's because experience teaches us that a love-up is the hero's just reward. Maybe it's because the tears provide us with a chance to catch up on the moments we missed with our children. Maybe it's because a breakdown is exactly what we want them to feel when we're inside them, turning like tornados, collapsing them with overwhelming force.

But I've never analysed it — even now — which means I didn't analyse it that night. In the moment I just knew I wanted to hold her close and tell her what she needed to hear to make the crying stop, whatever that might have been… to make her pull herself together, to make her feel the world was alright, to hold her, perhaps, as I wished I'd held Pierre the last time he cried before he made that leap of faith, chancing that there had to be a better place on the other side of life.

"It's going to be OK," I whispered, in the way I should have whispered to my own sweet boy. And before I knew it, I'd held my arms towards her and she'd stood and come towards me and I'd held her close. She was heavy in my arms, as if her legs had lost their strength to fully hold her up, and her body shook and trembled like there wasn't just a single Chloe in her floral dress but several Chloes rolling round and crawling round, scrounging for a place where they could rest, could fit, be safe, find home.

"Your boy wants to talk to you," she said through tears. "He wants to connect with you. He trusts me cause I've been to the other side. He sent me here to you."

By then she was no longer Chloe to me. The more I held her and thought of Pierre, the more I felt her changing into him, the more I needed her to be him, for my sake, just so I could tell him that I loved him, that I loved him so, and that it was my fault, my fault, my frigging fault for not trying harder to know, to feel, to understand, to accept, to protect, to soothe, to query, to challenge, to fight, to encourage, to permit.

"Oh my boy," I whispered. "Oh my sweet boy. It's OK. You can tell me anything. Anything. You have my ear. My ear and my heart belong to you."

"First of all," she said, "your son wants you to know that he is in a place of incredible beauty. So beautiful that he finds it hard to describe. You would never believe it. More than that, he is surrounded by a group of loving, intelligent souls who are taking care of him, so you should not be worrying about where he is or what is happening to him. He's fine. He's more than fine. He's happy."

I wanted to let her go. Her words felt inauthentic. She was struggling with the role. But I held her still. She was all I had. My blasted son was dead.

"Thank you," I told her. "Thank you. Thank you, darling. Thank you."

"Next, he wants you to stop beating up yourself with guilt. What happened was meant to happen." I eased my hold on her. Fear rushed in between us, and I squeezed her tightly once again.

"No. No. No," I said. "Don't say that. Don't say that. No, son. It was not supposed to happen. That's not how it's supposed to be at all. You were supposed to grow old and carry my casket to my grave and cry for me, my love, then smile as you claimed your inheritance, all the things I left for you — the shoes in which I married your mother, the life insurance payback, the playbills signed by Derek Walcott, the house on the hillside in Dominica, all my artwork, the steel penknife which my father said had cut the tangled ropes on one of the *Titanic's* lifeboats, all the old kaiso LPs, my personally autographed copy of *Giovanni's Room*."

I began to find it hard to breathe. Like I was holding her too hard. It was fear. Fear like a blade trying to get between us. Like wind prying shingles from a roof. A car had backfired on the plain and I'd been yanked out of the movie I was making in my mind, the one in which I was the loving father cradling his son, and the sounds of the world rushed inside my head… a mix of heartbeat, music, tree frogs, crickets, wind, distant human voice… and I became aware of myself as I was, a desperate man holding a broken woman whom he wanted to die and come back as his son.

I saw myself like I was not myself, but another Irving watching from above. Or so I wanted to think. So I wanted to believe. And I willed myself to believe it, and as soon as I did this, I could ask her to speak of him.

"Pierre," I whispered, "if you're here, let me know. Are you here?" A hand slipped up my back and cupped my head. A voice said, "Yes."

"How do I know?"

"It's me. Yes it's me."

"Me who?"

"Daddy?"

"Yes, son?"

"No. It's not Daddy. It's not Daddy."

"Yes, it's me. Yes it's me."

"No it's not Daddy."

"Yes, Pierre. It's me. Please believe me. It's me."

"It's not Daddy. It's not Daddy. It's Dad."

"God bless you. God bless you. God bless you, my son. Yes. God bless you. Yes. It's Dad."

"Dad? Dad?"

"Yes. Pierre."

"I love you, Dad. Stop worrying. It's over. Don't bother to try and live for me. You can't live for me. Move on with your life. It's over, Dad. It's finished. It's done."

I stood there holding Chloe for a very long time. How long, I'm not sure But long enough for Pelham and Tina to feel they had to come and find me.

It was an awkward scene: Chloe and I were hugging each other in silence with our eyes closed, rubbing each other's back, crying when crying would come, quiet when the quiet brought relief, but not talking, not talking. Then, in the middle of this search for peace, I heard Tina calling from a distance and Pelham coughing to warn me.

"I think we getting ready," Tina shot from thirty yards away. She was angry for sure. When I looked, she was already tramping up the grade. Pelham was squatting with his elbows on his thighs and moving his head from side to side as if he had to double check what he had seen. Before he left, he clapped his hands and laughed.

"So you're gone?" Chloe said composing herself.

I began to do the same. "Yes, I gone."

"Thanks for holding me."

In a mutter, I said, "No. Thank you." And somehow I knew that I'd return to Kingston as a slightly different man. Different how and to what degree, I didn't know. But I knew.

"Be good," Chloe said, and kissed her palm. She placed it on my cheek.

"I will," I mumbled, "I hope to see you again."

"Some things you should leave in their time," she said.

"You're right, you know. That's true."

"You're not coughing anymore," she said brightly.

I touched my throat. "I only cough when I smoke," I said, and smiled.

"But you don't do that anymore."

"How do you know that?"

"I know a lot of things," she said, and shooed me off. I realised then that she was wearing bangles. They clattered when they shook.

As I walked up the grade towards the house, I turned to look at her again. She was lighting up a spliff.

"He never used to call me *Daddy*, you know," I shouted. "He only used to call me *Dad*."

"I know."

"I was going to ask you how you know, but I think I know. Or at least I know what I want to know."

"You know," she said, "you're just putting up a fight."

"How you know?"

"Because," she said, "I know."

She was veiled in smoke. I could see the glow and smell the spliff burning fierce and new. My last impression was a shadow in a swirl of smoke dissolving in the glimmer of the city's lights.

(*2006*)

Showdown In Bridgetown

1.30pm

No matter how you want to look at it, there's something downright disturbing, strange and incongruous to see a young man in a well-fitted, grey suit and carrying a black briefcase, running from building to building in the gnawing heat of the Bajan Sun at midday. It was downright weird and disconcerting, especially as his right hand formed an imaginary gun ready to fire at time. Because of that, some of his friends attempted to nickname him "Django." He loved the idea; to him, it was cool, real cool and sexy. Also, he liked the way the "D" disappeared when pronounced —'Jango — just as how his pretend character vanished when he was not in cowboy mode. So, the nickname didn't stick.

His real name was Leroy Labad, a Dominican final-year student in Administrative Management, who we knew behaved normally, except around exam time when it was considered quite normal for almost everyone to get a little cranky. He was convinced that he was in for a showdown with the Sun. It was a game that he and the Sun had invented when he was just a little kid in Dominica. His vivid imagination allowed him to develop this personal relationship with the Sun and Rain that, even as an adult, saved him from boredom. It was for this reason he regretted not having bought himself a vehicle (or even an umbrella) upon his arrival in Barbados five years before.

"The lucky ole Sun had nothing to do but start a personal

vendetta with him," he thought. He lurked in the shadow of the library building, one of the largest on the UWI Cave Hill campus, waiting for some huge, cumulous clouds to give him some cover, then counted down the seconds: 4…3…2…1: 'Now!' he shouted to himself then sprinted onto the circular lawn. As he crossed the lawn, the sun emerged and once more bared down upon him. With the sun in hot pursuit, he dashed into the Administrative Building where his girlfriend, Kim Fisher, worked. Heads turned as he pushed through the glass doors of the air-conditioned building. They had never seen him in a suit before. African dashikis were more his style. But he had lived in Barbados long enough to know what was and what was not acceptable by the various levels of society. So, he had even trimmed down his Afro hairstyle by two inches He acknowledged the staff's smiles and nods of approval by flashing them one of his best Hollywood sparklers, while pointing to the African pattern on his tie, and mock pleading for forgiveness.

His performance was interrupted when he looked down the central aisle to see Kim, rushing up to him and certainly not smiling. Kim was a pretty girl, with curves in all the right places. She was smart too and knew how to get things done. When they had met each other two years earlier it was love at first sight and they did make a handsome couple, truth be told.

Kim pulled him aside, towards a vacant desk near the glass doors, then gently and respectfully brought his face about two inches from hers so he could see her irises adjusting their focus. Then she said, "Leroy, do you have an important meeting this afternoon?"

"Yes" he replied.

"And at what time is that meeting scheduled for?"

"3.00pm," he replied.

"And do you know what the time is now, Mr Wolf?"

"Time to go get the two o'clock bus to Bridgetown."

She turned towards the staff members seated close enough to follow the developing drama.

"He sweet, eh," she said to her fast-growing audience of stenographers leaving their desks to get a better position to pick up the finest details of this real live soap opera.

"What's the matter with you, Leroy?" she continued. Two drops of perspiration rolled down his left arm.

Leroy was taken off-guard. "I was..."

"OK", she said cutting him off, and putting on the demeanour of a mother preparing her little baby boy going to pre-school for the first time.

"Here's your briefcase with everything in it: your dossier outlining all your academic and extra-curricula achievements; the completed questionnaire; a note with your name on it, which you should read as soon as you get on the bus, and a CONFIDENTIAL letter to Mr Trenton — which you must hand deliver to him just before the meeting begins. Timing is very important; and a wedding anniversary card addressed to Aunty Lily, and another wedding anniversary card addressed to Uncle Singay both containing $25.00 which you are to give to them. Aunty Lily and Uncle Singay may be on the two o'clock bus. If not, they will wait for you at the entrance of Mr Trenton's offices. But don't worry, everything will be alright. JUST GO! NOW!"

"Wah?? Hold on, hold on!" exclaimed Leroy.

"I said everything will be OK. Now hurry down to the bus stop before you miss the two o'clock."

"But..."

"No time for that now, Leroy. Go on! NOW!!!"

Leroy squeezed her hand and smiled. "OK. Will call you tonight," he said as he hurried out of the building on to the sizzling road, taking off his jacket as he did so. Luckily, the Sun seemed to be having his siesta and was hidden behind the clouds again but that did not stop the heat from baring down on him.

The bus stop was only a four minute walk away, but it seemed much further today. "Damn those buses! The gods are certainly not with me today," he mumbled to himself as he noted that there was no bus in sight. He glanced down at his watch — a birthday gift from Kim — and realised he was going to be late for his 3.00pm interview with Trenton Engineering Corp in their spanking new offices in Bridgetown.

He knew he was well qualified for the advertised post which offered a salary that would allow him to pay back his student loan with ease. Going back home to Dominica where jobs were so scarce was not an option. He was comfortable here in "Bimshire" with his Bajan girlfriend, Saturday night drive-in movies and Sundays on Accra Beach with friends to ease the tension of the work week. The year was 1975, he was twenty-three, and the world was his oyster. But right now it was on the blinking bus which was nowhere to be seen nor was it coming round the corner to pick him up and deposit him at the gates of what he hoped would become his personal "Magic Kingdom": Trenton Engineering Corp.

Suddenly one of those huge red monster buses came noisily around the corner. Leroy's heartbeat rose for a moment — but no. This was a Grazettes bus; it would not do. It passed without stopping filled with jabbering schoolchildren, some of whom made funny faces at him, then burst out laughing as it sped away. Leroy looked at his watch:

2.25pm
Those unruly school children out already! I will never make it to the interview. But no sooner had he thought this when he noticed something coming round the corner. He put his arm out without quite looking at the bus itself. On raising his head, he could not believe what he saw. Approaching him in slow motion and emerging from a cloud of coloured smoke was not a bus, but a

fantasy interpretation of four types of Bajan public transport from over the past century or so. First came two beautiful donkeys decorated in gold and red, pulling along their dray cart. Next came a downsized "Pick-Up" bus with its seat benches, followed by the all too familiar school bus, and finally a modern ZR bus with its spectacular murals depicting community life and local heroes. The total assemble of these glittering colours was too much for the Bajan Sun who slipped behind a mango tree.

Above the windscreen of the Pick-Up bus was a large banner saying Barbados Fine Rums presents A Tribute to Public Transportation in the City — Crop-Over 1986. Seated on a pedestal at the back of the bus was — you guessed it — Aunty Lily and Uncle Singay, resplendent in their Crop-Over costumes. Rhythmic Barbadian calypsos had everyone in the bus swaying and dancing.

"Leroy, come quick! Jump on! You going to be late for your interview." Aunty Lily called out. Leroy who appeared to have been immobilised by this apparition shook himself alive and dashed to the back of the Pick-Up.

"Come in m' chile," said a Fat Woman sitting on the edge of the seat at the open back of the Pick-Up. At the same time, she yanked Leroy's jacket and briefcase from him. "Look May, hol' dis bag and jacket fuh de young fella," she said, passing them to May, who passed them to a man further inside the covered wooden benches, who I will call "Lazy Man". Then she suddenly held on to Leroy's arm and tugged him violently into the bus. Leroy barely had time to shoot his hands out to prevent himself from crashing into the benches and the people sitting on them.

"Thank you," he said more out of habit than of any genuine feeling of gratitude.

"Er… can I have my briefcase and jacket back, please?"

"Sure," replied the lady who immediately turned to Lazy Man, who grabbed the briefcase and jacket from him and passed them to Leroy with a broad grin. "Any time darling."

Just then the Sun reappeared from behind the tree, but he was too late. Leroy was safe and sound, shaded from him and — on his way to Bridgetown at top speed. Leroy then opened the briefcase, took out the letter addressed to himself and read it. It was a list of possible questions the board members could ask him, which he and Kim had gone through several times already. With a short "chups", he slipped the note back into the briefcase and looked at his watch.

2.40pm

"Happy Anniversary," Leroy said.

"Thank you," Lily replied. "As you can see, we are celebrating in style. I is the pretend Queen and Singay is the real King".

Everybody laughed.

The week before, Leroy had met the couple at Kim's home where they gave him their family history. They had separated twice, and Singay had gone to prison once for being drunk and disorderly. Their children were all married and lived in the USA and the UK. Lily and Singay had been living in England some 35 years and had returned home five years ago. "We trying to fit in," Lily said.

"Broad Street, Bridgetown," shouted the driver. "End of the line, everybody out!"

"What!" shouted Fat Woman. "That's the fastest I ever reach to town. And onna Crop Over afternoon to boot!"

Leroy looked at his watch in surprise. "2:45pm! I made it! Maybe it's true what they say time does go faster in a carnival!"

He then turned to Lily and Singay and said, "I have a surprise for y'all."

He quickly opened the briefcase and removed the two envelopes addressed to them.

"From Kim and I," he said as he handed them each their

envelope and slid out of the bus. "Have a great day. And careful, hear, there's money in there."

"We know." They both laughed.

"Uncle, remember to behave yourself," Leroy called out.

"I will make sure he does," Aunty Lily replied

Leroy waved goodbye to them and walked quickly into the air-conditioned coolness and quiet of the front desk of Trenton Engineering Corp where he was greeted by a pretty, immaculately groomed receptionist in a tight grey outfit.

2.55pm

"Mr Labad, I assume." She flashed a wide bright smile at him.

"Correct." He smiled back just as broadly.

"I am Janet Weekes, Mr Trenton's personal secretary. We had sent you a questionnaire to fill out and bring with you today. Mr Trenton will need to look at it before he interviews you. Do you have it?"

"Of course." Leroy opened the briefcase, retrieved the completed form, and handed it to her.

"Have a seat, I'll be back in a while," she said. "Two of the board members are late so you have time to relax. The restroom is this way if you want to use it."

Leroy thanked her, went to the restroom, freshened up at the sink and then opened his briefcase removing the "Private and Confidential" letter for Mr Trenton from it. He then realised that the letter was not sealed. "What? Papa Bon Dieu!" he said to himself. "What trial you sending 'dere for me this afternoon nuh?" Reverting to Dominican dialect in distress. On an impulse he removed the letter from the envelope and began to read it.

"Hi Baby. Man, I miss you so much. And yes, I do remember that I owe you a "favour". Perhaps I can make up for it this weekend. There are so many great Crop Over fetes all over the place. I am happy to see that my nephew from Dominica has made it as one of the finalists for the vacancy at your office. I would be so glad if you could help him get through. He's a genius and will most likely walk away with all the awards this year.

"Yes! I know, the Dominica accent! But don't worry, he learns very fast. Last week I heard him pronouncing television as 'televigeon'. He loves our sweet Bajan lingo. Oh oh, that would mean that I owe you two favours! I cannot wait to give them to you. Give me a call if we can meet any time soon."

Love, Love, Love

Kim"

"Look at my crosses here dis afternoon!" Leroy thought angrily as he finished reading the letter. He was staring fixedly at it when he was startled by a knock on the door of the restroom.

"Mr Labad," Mrs Weekes called out, "Mr Trenton is ready for you."

3.15pm

He shakily folded the letter, replaced it into the envelope, and sealed it. As he returned to the front desk, a gentleman entered the lobby, the secretary turned and smiled. "Mr Trenton this is Mr Labad, the last of the candidates to be interviewed."

"Mr Labad pleased to meet you. We almost gave up on you, but you are right on time. Let's go to the boardroom." Leroy handed him the letter from Kim as the three of them proceeded to the boardroom saying, "I was asked to deliver this to you."

"By whom?" asked Mr Trenton.

"By the principal's secretary," replied Leroy.

The deafening silence of the anteroom they entered was ominous, grim. But when Mr Trenton put his little finger on the shining golden latch, the two massive sliding doors drew apart, like the old Rock of Sesame herself, and the silence of the anteroom was replaced by raucous laughter coming from the board members who were munching hors d'oeuvres and sipping glasses of wine and other liquid delights.

Trenton who had just finished reading the letter handed to him, took his seat at the head of the table. He took a sip from his wine glass as he glanced around the table. He then nodded to Mrs Weekes who called the meeting to order. As the members took their seats, Trenton sneaked Leroy a sly grin and the meeting began.

Before anyone realised it, Leroy was being interviewed with questions being fired at him from all directions, including questions about why he wanted to work in Barbados instead of St Lucia. Leroy was able to answer succinctly and clarified that he was from Dominica not St Lucia. His answers drew grunts of approval from the board members and before he could catch his breath, the interview was over. His terms of employment and salary had been discussed as well as other details of employment. At the end Leroy was given a resounding round of applause. There was much handing shaking and back patting as the board members filed out of the boardroom.

Mr Trenton and Leroy were among the last to leave. Leroy picked up the sweet soca rhythm now coming from the boardroom and did a little chip-chip on the way to the front entrance. By that time almost everyone had made it to their cars and were already driving out of the parking lot two floors below.

4.15pm

Laughing as they left the building, Mr Trenton asked, "How are you getting home, Leroy?"

"Same way I came, Sir, by minibus," he replied. "I am just going past Speights Town."

Laughing, Mr Trenton said, "Oh, that's on my way, lucky bastard, I'll give you a lift."

No one heard the Mercedes arrive. It simply arrived like a whisper, or a midday drizzle on a sunny day. The Driver then stepped out of the car and opened the back door for Mr Trenton. Leroy paused then opened the front passenger door. Mr Trenton stopped him. "No, no, no," he called out. "Please join me here in the back."

He then turned to the Driver and said, "Leroy, this is Mr Gittens — better known as Gittens, and Gittens this is Mr Labad. From Grenada. He will be joining the firm next week. We are giving him a lift home now."

He paused for a moment as he remembered his own story which was not unlike Leroy's own today. 'Arrives by Minibus, and goes home in a Mercedes!'

"Congratulations, Sir," Gittens said as soon as Leroy got into the car.

Mr Trenton turned to Leroy and said, "You did very well."

"Thank you, Sir" he replied. "I had many sleepless nights trying to decide if I should stay here in Barbados or go back home to… Where do I come from again?"

"Dominica?" the Boss asked.

"Yeh. Correct." They both shouted and laughed.

As the laughter simmered down, Leroy continued, "But seriously now, the world is changing, the Caribbean is coming into its own. Dominica is scheduled for independence in three years…"

"By that time, you will have learnt enough from us and will have developed good contacts regionally and internationally, you will see."

"You know our population is only 85,000 people, Sir. A sovereign state! That has to be a joke! However, Jesus started with twelve."

The Boss retorted, "But, his father had lots of friends in high places!"

Both of them laughed.

4.35pm

Suddenly the car swerved barely missing a Pick-Up bus, filled with passengers, that cut across in front of the Mercedes. There was much singing, dancing and drinking on the bus. Leroy recognised it as the same advertising float minus the donkeys, with Aunty Lily, Uncle Singay, their group of friends, and others not in costume.

"Goblimey!" exclaimed Gittens.

"Boy that was close!" the Boss answered.

Leroy shook his head. "Crop Over in de air! Fete tonight!"

"Speights Town people boy, you know any of them?" asked the Boss.

"Nearly all of them," Leroy replied. "Oh Lord, see how the bus overtaking everybody like a hot knife in butter."

Just then one police car, siren blaring, overtook them followed by two police motor bikes. The traffic slowly came to a halt. Leroy took a deep breathe, looking out of the window at the commotion on the shoulder of the highway up ahead, with the passengers of the Pick-Up Bus, the driver and the police in a heated argument.

He sighed deeply, and said, "Sir, no offence meant but I need to go and check out what the problem is."

"Sure man, I am not going anywhere anyway." He opened his newspaper as Leroy and the driver got out of the car and approached the group.

"Officers, what seems to be the problem here?" Gittens asked.

"This group of persons are making a nuisance of themselves and distracting the driver causing him to drive erratically."

The familiar high-pitched voice of Aunty Lily suddenly broke over the commotion. "That not true Leroy, no driver driving erratically. We just enjoying ourselves on the bus."

Singay cut in, "Actually we just sipping a little spirits, to celebrate our fifty years."

"What! And the driver drinking too? That's a criminal offence you know!" replied one of the policemen.

"Dat not true. The driver not drinking."

"Where he is. Bring him here! Bring him here!"

The driver was brought forward, and was asked to walk a straight line, which he did with ease.

Mr Trenton who by that time was getting bored, looked across the seat and saw Leroy's briefcase. He checked to see where Leroy was and quickly pulled the briefcase towards him and opened it. He looked through the papers and was about to close back the briefcase when he saw the edge of a photograph among the documents. He pulled it out. It was a beautiful black and white photograph of Kim. He turned it over and read 'Lots of Love, Kim'. He put the photograph in the inside pocket of his jacket, closed the briefcase, smiled, shut his eyes and leaned back in his seat.

5.30pm

Back on the sidewalk the policemen decided that the driver was indeed sober and agreed to let him go with a warning. Leroy suggested that the police allowed the bus to drive on the sidewalk to get into the parking lot along the beach. With the blaring of horns and shouting from the frustrated motorists, the police agreed.

"By the way, where is the rest of the float for the Parade?" asked Leroy.

"Oh," Lily answered, "they will be on the road tomorrow. Is over twenty of them."

"So how come is just ounu on the road now?" Leroy asked.

"Mistake nuh man. They bring the schedule for us and give it to Singay and he mix up the dates," Lily said.

"That means wunna will be on the road tomorrow?"

"Of course," Singay cut in.

Leroy asked Gittens to tell the Boss that he would stay with the group to ensure that there were no further incidents. Gittens returned to the car and delivered the message.

"The traffic will be moving in a few minutes," he said, "I will just hand him his jacket and briefcase as we pass by."

As the driver handed Leroy his belongings, the Boss wound down the window and said with a smile, "I thought you told me you don't like politics!"

"Politics!" Leroy said, "Nah man. Just going to have a drink with the comrades and celebrate my success with them for a while."

"Ha ha, no politics, no politics! Yeh right Comrade!" laughed the Boss as they drove off.

6.14pm

As the bus moved the few feet to the beach, the driver turned up the music and shouted, "Ladies and Gentlemen, it is party time! Drinks on the house!" The true spirit of Crop Over took over.

As Leroy removed his tie and placed them over his briefcase and jacket, Lily handed him a rum and coke.

"She showed you what I gave her for the anniversary?" Singay asked.

"What! You get present too, come leh me see it!" Lily shook her head to show Leroy her new gold earrings.

"What Singay, you have good taste man!" Leroy said as they slapped hands.

"That's my Sweet Boy!" Lily said, "Come guys a little dance on that."

Leroy said, "Go on man enjoy yourself, I'll come in a little while."

6:30pm

With his rum and coke in hand, Leroy strolled onto the beach where he found a fallen tree that had formed itself into a most comfortable seat. He sat down, took a sip from his glass, and turned towards the setting Sun just in time to catch the Sun's final bullet, the illusive Green Flash. He jumped back and hid behind the driftwood. He slowly got up and checked to see if everyone was OK. Of course, no one had noticed the green flash of the bullet, they were too busy enjoying De Red Plastic Bag's current soca hit. As he sat back down on the log, a pretty young lady, whom he had noticed when he got back on the bus, came up to him, handed him another drink, and sat next to him.

"Are you the one they called Django?" she asked.

"Yes, Django, that's me," he replied. They both turned to the beautiful afterglow of the Sun. Leroy swore the cloud formation looked very much like a cowboy on horseback, riding into the sunset.

(2020)

A Toothbrush For Christmas

I shot up from my bed on the first beat of the Goat Skin Drummers. The clock on the night table said 5.45am and the calendar next to it, December 24, 1958 — MY TENTH BIRTHDAY! With a smile stretching from ear to ear, I rushed towards the veranda using my newly acquired authority to wake my big brother, Calvin, and my cousins, Gregory and Mickey, all still asleep.

"Everybody wake up!" I shouted. "Nine Morning band coming 'round the corner!"

"What?... Jeff?...," drooled Calvin, trying to catch his bearings. My parents' alarm clock answered him with a loud RRRRRR RRRR-inggggggg.

"The Nine Morning band," I repeated. "Today is Christmas Eve! Come fellas! Let's get on the veranda before those girls."

Mama had started her usual wake-up knock against the partition. "Hurry! They're on our street already," Mama shouted, running through the passage to the veranda to join my sister Mara and cousins Colette and Fay who had slyly beat us to the best seats. Dad followed with a tray full of hot cacao tea.

"The Lapo Kabwit sweet, eh!," Mama sang out while doing a fancy three-step to the music. In the glow of the dim street lamps, the band of revellers morphed into a sea of writhing, billowing tides and currents, mesmerising and hypnotic, like the Roseau River in spate.

"Drink you rum on a Christmas morning, drink, you rum," the

happy band sang in chorus. "Mama drink if you drinking!" The Chantwel, a small-bodied, spritely little woman with a voice louder than a microphone, challenged the crowd's response as she danced backwards facing them. They replied with equal gusto: "Drink you rum on a Christmas morning, drink you rum."

I can remember visualising the revellers pulling a reluctant sun over Morne Anglais as they chipped down King George V Street. In my vivid imagination I could see puffs of cloud rolling down the dew-drenched mountainside releasing showers of liquid sunshine to wash Roseau's streets and gutters clean for this bright new day.

Mama looked at the rising sun with trepidation. "Sun rising fast; have rain in it too," she warned, looking up the Roseau Valley. "That means we'll have to move fast to get all the Christmas chores done."

"That's why we came to help you, Aunty," said Colette.

"Well I am so glad to hear that because..." She pulled a long sheet of paper from her front pocket. "I have them all listed here, ready to be assigned to our teams." The boys heaved a collective grand sigh.

"I know," Mama said gently. "But remember, many hands make work light."

"Too many cooks spoil the broth," Calvin hissed dryly.

Mama ignored that and carried on gallantly. "Here's the list," she said, as she distributed copies to everyone giving detailed instructions as to how the tasks should be completed. I was the first to protest. "All that in one day?" I shouted.

"Mr Jeffrey, you will please raise your hand if you have a question!" Mama retorted. "But Mama," I continued, "I was planning to do some of my Christmas shopping this morn..."

"Mr Jeffrey, I agreed for your cousins to come and spend Christmas with us in town only if you all agreed to pull your weight and work quickly and efficiently. Calvin, Gregory, and

Mickey, you all remember that?"

"Yes Mama," we replied sheepishly.

"Yes Sir, Ma'am, Boss, Captain, Sergeant…" said everyone bursting out laughing. Everyone, except me. I sat down to read my long job description. "That's still too much," I shouted again. But the others gave me so ferocious a cut-eye that I shut up and dragged myself off to my first assignment asking everyone if slavery was still legal in the West Indies.

Mama heard me and simply said, "You want to leave early? Start early. Or get one or two of your "enslaved" friends in the neighbourhood to help you."

"But it's my birthday," I said to myself. "Nobody remembering that?" I tried to hold back the tears that were welling up in my eyes as I walked away. But it was Cousin Colette who asked the Million Dollar Question after breakfast. "An what is this Red Toothbrush at the bottom of the list?" she asked.

Mama did a double take, an then said, "Oh, …am…that was just a slip. Not meant for you all at all. Look, sun up, so have your breakfast and let's get going." Then turning to Dad, she said, "Come Henry, we have our share to do!" Dad shook his head and followed her into the house.

Mama told me later, that, as she walked off with Dad, she had a strong premonition that trouble was afoot. It didn't take long! As we were finishing breakfast, Gregory asked, "So, what is the real story behind the red toothbrush?"

"Christmas, for my mother," I answered, "means, among several other traditions, the purchasing of a new red toothbrush, usually from the Dominica Dispensary, and always in the last five minutes before all the shops shut their doors. It is basically a superstition she got from her grandmother, and if she does not get that particular toothbrush, she believes that bad luck will follow her for the entire new year."

"And you believe that too?" Calvin asked.

"Umm," I replied, smiled, and moved off to begin my chores, my head dizzy in anticipation of the joys of Shopping Day. I could see myself in Roseau on Christmas Eve when the commercial sector turned into a playground filled with cars and trucks; children in their Sunday best taking home toy cars, trucks and dolls of all descriptions; and homemade sweets like coconut cheese, tablet *haché*, tamarind balls, and unbreakable. And how, when the shop lights came on the excitement went a pitch higher with kids running up and down with squeals of delight as they waved starlight sparklers and called out to each other; and mothers warning them to look out for the bigger boys tossing mini bombs at the feet of passersby; vendors hawking their merchandise; and a Santa or two whining their waist to some catchy Christmas calypso to the great amusement of everyone.

It all ended at ten o'clock, when the shops closed their doors and shopkeepers and shoppers drifted off to their homes and churches for their midnight services. But I began to realise that this year I might not be part of that scene at all, given the number of assignments that lay before me.

At about eleven o'clock that morning, disaster struck! Mama was in the kitchen when Calvin shouted from upstairs, "Ma? Ma? The lino for the passage is too short."

"Well go back to the store and tell them to cut an extra piece for you. Is ten feet I told them not nine," said Ma.

"Been there, done that," said Gregory, Mickey and I together.

"They hadn't got more in that colour," said Mickey. "It finish!"

"No more of the design or the colour?" asked Ma sensing another problem arising.

"Go and see for yourself," said Gregory.

"Look boy, don't be rude to me! I'm your Aunty!"

"Sorry Aunty."

"Look, take this money and go by Red Store and see if they have it."

"Too late. It finish there too," Mickey and I said in unison.

"Look, go to your father and tell him what happen. He will know how to handle that problem," said Mama as she turned to speak with Zabet, the cook.

Upstairs in the drawing-room, the girls were having no better luck. The two dried coconut husks used for polishing the floor were apparently too old and were falling apart in the girls' small but tough hands.

"And the Christmas Tree fall down," chimed in Miss Fay.

"But nofing don't break," Mara added.

"Well if you say so…" said Colette.

"Something break self!" said Fay, "the big star at the top. And all the lights stop lighting!"

"Not true!" said Mara.

"True!" said Fay.

"Not true!" said Mara.

"She lying!" said Fay.

"Who lying dere?" said Mara.

"OK, OK," Mama interjected. "The boys will fix it when they come back. Right now, I want to see everybody in the yard by the pond in ten seconds, starting now… Mikey where you going?"

"Nowhere," he replied.

"How you mean nowhere? I see you coming from under the mango tree where we boiling the ham," Mama said, growing more concerned with every second.

"Oh," said Mickey, "I was just checking my bird."

"Bird? What bird?" Mama asked.

"Dis morning I put a bird to boil with de ham," he replied, "they say it will give each other flavour."

"What! You put it alive with all its feathers! Everything?" Mama shouted.

"Yes… but it's dead now," Mickey replied.

"Dead now! Well your backside going and come alive when

your Uncle give you a few hot ones..." Mama screamed. "Everybody upstairs. I re-assigning all of you. But wait… where is Jeffrey?"

"He go and get Eugene to help us," Mickey replied.

"Wait, who you say?" Mama asked.

"Eugene," repeated Colette.

"Father in Heaven! Not Eugene!" Mama said with growing agitation.

"The mad boy from America?" asked Mara.

"Mad?" said Mama. "He more than mad! Last week he fall and roll down the front step ten times, saying he is John Wayne dodging bullets in a saloon shoot out. And is only because he burst his mouth on the tenth time that he stop! I don't want him here again at all, at all!" Mama said.

"Well, too late. Here he comes!" Calvin exclaimed. All eyes immediately turned to the gate as we hear Eugene's voice shouting in a rank Brooklyn accent, "Come on, Come in. Nobody gonna hurt you."

Eugene with three unknown boys and I march into the yard. "You see that dere? That's a pond. But for today this is the Rio Grandé because it is Christmas Eve. Now first, I'm going to show you how John Wayne survives an Indian attack in the River Grandé. I'm going to be John Wayne. Now let us see who's going to be the Indian Chief… OK you — the tall one — you're gonna be the Indian chief. Pull out a gun and shoot me."

Out of nowhere, Mama comes running, "No, no, no, NO shooting. Nobody is going to be shot in this pond today."

"It is not a pond," says Eugene. "It's the Rio Grandé!"

"Whatever," says Mama.

But Tall Boy doesn't hear her. His hands go up slowly. "Bang," he says, pointing his finger like a gun. The other boys immediately join in, and the shooting frenzy ensues "Pow, Bang, Bang, Pow." Eugene turns around slowly, looks at the Indian chief, puts up his hand to say something but the words don't come. He begins to tremble, his whole body shaking till he can stand no more. He freezes, his legs buckle under him and he falls into the pond with a tremendous belly-splash, drenching everyone. A huge howl of admiration followed by hooting and clapping ensued. They look to the pond, but Eugene is nowhere to be seen in its murky green waters. Twenty seconds go by, no Eugene. Thirty seconds, no Eugene. Thirty five seconds, no Eugene. Mama can take it no more. She jumps into the pond and searches around for Eugene. She finds him, pulls him up and jams him against the wall. "What on earth are you trying to do? Drive me crazy?" she screeches.

Eugene says, "Oh man! What you do dat for? Now you spoilt everything. I was just about to make my grand revival and end this battle by killing the Indian Chief and his men. Now I am going to have to start all over ag…"

"OH NO. NO!" Mama shouted. "YOU are going to make a grand EXIT. Right now, all of you, OUT! The rest of you upstairs! You are all in punishment. Nobody is going anywhere until shopping time at five o'clock."

"We?" says Gregory. "But we didn't do nothing."

"You clapped," Mama snapped. "You encouraged him. That's it. Everybody out!"

Eugene left quickly with his gang, we ran upstairs to wait for five o'clock. But that was not all. Just as Mama began mixing her cakes there was a knock on the door. Mama answered it. It was Miss Johnson from the cathedral choir. "Mrs B," she said. "Miss Evadney Richards say she cannot sing *Minuit Chrétien* tonight. She is leaving the church. And Mr Francis Toulon has the flu and he can hardly talk."

There was a long silence. Mama eventually asks, "So?"

"You will have to do it", says Miss Johnson.

"But it is in French", says Mama. "I don't know it in French."

"Neither does most of the congregation," whispers Miss

Johnson with a sly little smile. Both women look to the sky, then Mrs Johnson says, "Tell you what, we will type out the French version for you. You speak French creole, don't you? Well, all you have to do is add some choice creole words in appropriate places and belt it loud on the chorus. I am sure that will work, don't worry. Rehearsal is from 2-3pm. See you there. Bye." She turned quickly and disappeared down the street.

Mama sent Gregory to call her sister to take over the cake making while she went to the rehearsal. All the other traditions were observed including us children licking the bowl and spoon used to make the cake.

Mama made it to work on time and her employer even gave her time off to go and buy her traditional toothbrush fifteen minutes before closing time. But, alas, it was too late. There were no red toothbrushes left on the rack. Mama was heartbroken. When she finally dragged herself home from work and recalled how her whole day was ruined, how badly the rehearsal had gone, and especially not having her red toothbrush for the first time since she had started the habit, she thought that she could just put her head in her hands and cry. Luckily for her, though, her cakes had just come back from Jake's Bakery and the house was full of the sweet aroma of hot Christmas cake. So, she got up, emptied two bottles of sherry over the cakes, cut herself a huge slice from the biggest cake, sat on the edge of her bed and as she was about to eat it, I walked in.

"Mama, you crying?" I asked.

"Yes," she said, biting into a huge chunk of cake. "What else can I do? My whole day has been a total disaster and I didn't even wish you Happy Birthday or let you know how proud we are of you. Here have some cake." I bit into the warm cake, with its wine-drenched fruits — oh that glorious taste of Christmas!

Mama continued, "Your father arranged a special gift for you. He hired the Union Club for your birthday party tomorrow,

Christmas Day. All your friends will be there. We are going to have a goooood time. Lots of food, music and presents." I hugged her and, with tears streaming down our faces, we began laughing.

Mama had never been so early for church in all her life. By 11.15, she and the six children were taking a leisurely walk up Constitution Hill when a squeaky voice shouted to her, "Mrs B can I have a word with you please?" Of course, it was Eugene. Mama sent us up the hill to wait for her and turned to him, "Yes Eugene, what is it now?" Eugene approached her with an envelope and gift box. "This is for you Mrs B." Mama opened the envelope and read his crabby handwriting: "Dear Mrs B, I apologise for my behaviour this afternoon. Please accept this small token of my respect for you. Signed Eugene."

She looked at the gift box. "Open it," said Eugene. Mama opened the box to find another long, slender box inside. She opened it to find a red toothbrush encased in an airtight glass tube. Mama gasped. "I found it at the bottom of the pond this afternoon. So, can we be friends?" asked Eugene. Mama is in tears. She hugs him. "Yes, Yes," she said.

"My Grandma says I can come to church with you, if you agree?"

"Of course," Mama answered. Eugene took a bow, offered his right arm to Mama, who took it, and the group walked regally into the cathedral.

After church, a number of friends and family came over to congratulate Mama on her beautiful rendition, including her old French teacher, who told her that her diction was so clear that this was the first time he realised the shepherds were having agouti broth when the angels appeared. The whole room burst into laughter. Then Dad put on his favourite Christmas music including "Drink your rum on a Christmas Morning..." and "Erica Wow oy Yow".

And so it was, that the gifting of red toothbrushes as symbols of family love and unity (not to mention good hygiene) began and spread to all the towns and villages around the island. Of course, Mr Eugene could not be outdone. Every year, he sends cartons of toothbrushes for Christmas to schools all over the world compliments Caribbean Stunts Inc., Hollywood, California. Each box contains a sheet describing how he and I set up Mama's surprise gift that year. I am sure that you too would like to know how that was done! But that's a different story!

(*2020*)